The Invisible Boy

Edwina Browne

The Invisible Boy

The Invisible Boy

Prologue

The noise in the small classroom was deafening – barking, snarling and choking sounds as the dog strained against its chain, desperately trying to lunge forward. The hair stood straight up on the back of its neck; ears pricked, and teeth bared – drool dripping from his jaws. His powerful shoulder muscles bulged, and his claws scraped against the wooden floor as he slipped and slid.

It took all of Agent Boyle's strength to hold him back. He gripped the leather handle of the lead with both hands, desperately trying to see what was provoking the dog. There was nothing in the room. Maybe it was a rat? But the dog was trained. He was their best police dog – a fearsome Alsatian to those on the wrong side of the law, but as gentle as a mouse once given the correct commands. He had never let them down before. Agent Boyle knew that the dog wouldn't act like this if it was merely a cat or a rat.

The dog's intelligent eyes were focussed intently at something in the far corner of the room, but Agent Boyle couldn't see anything. There was nothing there; it was just an empty corner.

An hour earlier, Agent Boyle had received a phone call from a policeman to say that something very unusual was happening in the local school.

"I can't say more over the phone," the police man had said. "But you must come urgently, or it might be gone!"

Now as he stood in the room with the dog, Agent Boyle could see that the police man had not been exaggerating.

There was something in the room.

"Show yourself or I'll set the dog on you," he called out, looking around for any sign of a disturbance. There was a silence for a minute and then to his complete surprise, a high-pitched voice came from the far side of the room.

"Okay, okay! Just stop the dog and I'll come over to you!"

Agent Boyle jumped, and stared intently where the voice had come from. He still couldn't see anything, but the voice sounded very real and life-like.

"Down, Rover!" he said.

The fearsome beast immediately lay down at his feet. His sharp ears continued to prick forward but his teeth were no longer bared – no more choking sounds, and he showed no sign of wanting to disobey his master.

In the sudden silence, Agent Boyle could hear a squeaking sound, like runners on a polished floor, but still there was nothing to be seen.

"Show yourself! Who are you?" he said, in a voice that sounded braver than he felt. His knuckles were white as he gripped the dog's chain tightly. It was not the first time that he was glad to have Rover at his side.

Agent Boyle wasn't a religious man, and he had never believed in the possibility that ghosts could exist and yet ... he had no explanation for the sounds that were coming from just a few feet in front of him. His cold blue eyes, normally narrow with suspicion, were wide as he stared around, and his heart beat unusually fast in his chest.

"I'm coming," said the same high-pitched voice, and this time he could tell that whatever it was, it was smaller than himself.

Agent Boyle reached out and swiped the air in front of him. To his surprise, his hand hit against something solid. He only just controlled himself enough to grip it tightly and not pull back in surprise. It felt soft and warm, like a small arm in a woollen jumper.

"Wha-what are you?" he stammered, desperately trying to see something –anything, that would indicate what it was that was in front of him.

Chapter 1

Two days earlier …

Peter woke with a jolt and looked around the dormitory. Everyone was sleeping peacefully but something had woken him. Something was on his mind.

He pushed his dark, floppy hair out of his eyes and squinted in the early morning rays as they crept weakly through the long windows. The gentle sounds of the boys breathing softly around him was all he could hear. Everything seemed normal. But he had a bad feeling in his stomach and that usually meant something was wrong. He lay back and put a pillow over his head, trying to go back to sleep. And then, his insides lurched as he remembered; he was in trouble. Billy, the bully in the class, and his enormous and permanently angry friend, Dean, had said that they were going to "get" him that day.

His exact words were, "I'm coming after you, Butt Brain. I'm going to get you."

It wasn't the actual words that concerned Peter – he had heard them many times before – it was *how* he said it that made Peter so uncomfortable. There was a viciousness in Billy's face that he hadn't seen before. A crazed fury that would have been unleashed immediately if he had been outside in the playground with no teachers to see him.

Peter knew that he shouldn't have called him "Rat Face" in front of all the boys, but it had certainly stopped the taunting, and it was so satisfying to see the surprise on Billy's face.

Ha! Peter had thought triumphantly at the time. *That will teach him!*

But it didn't seem like such a good idea now, as he lay in bed with a sick feeling in the pit of his stomach. He knew that Billy didn't like anyone mentioning how his buck teeth made him look like a rat, and now he would enlist Dean to help him get revenge. Peter lay there, tossing and turning, nervously thinking of the endless possibilities of how Billy could torment him.

There was a rustle from the next bed, and he turned over to see his friend Ronan beckoning to him.

"What's up, Peter? Are you okay?" he whispered.

"Not really," said Peter. "After what happened at breaktime yesterday, I'm in for it with Billy."

"Oh, yeah. That was a pretty stupid thing to say, all right. You should have ignored him."

"I couldn't resist it," said Peter. "It was just great to see the look on his face."

"Your big mouth always gets you into trouble."

"I know," sighed Peter. "And they're not the only ones I'm in trouble with today. Mr Grimes is going to kill me too."

The fifth class teacher in Peter's school was called Mr Grimes. He was a terrifying man – huge and fat, with bulging eyes that pointed in two different directions. Neither eye seemed to look directly at you, which made it very difficult to know which eye to focus on. If you focused on the left eye, it seemed that the right eye might have been a better choice, but then when you looked at the right eye, it was definitely looking at something far over to the right and behind you. To avoid confusion, Peter usually focused on his mouth instead. There was another reason for this. Mr Grimes always shouted when he spoke, and little flecks of spit shot out his mouth when he said any words beginning with a 'p' or a 'b', like 'Peter' or 'Bad Behaviour'. Peter thought that both of those words were going to be used frequently that day.

He looked enviously at Ronan's project which was neatly laid out on the table beside him. "I couldn't think of what to write for my project and I've nothing to hand in. I was even dreaming about Mr Grimes shouting at me last night."

"Maybe I can help you after breakfast," said Ronan, but there was a look of dismay on his face as his eyes fell on the almost blank sheet of paper on Peter's table. "Hmm… do you have anything more than that prepared?"

"Eh, I had a few ideas, but…"

A loud bang from the far end of the room interrupted the boys and they looked up with apprehension to see the large figure of Dean, bursting through the door and storming into the room.

"Up time! Up time!" he called, grinning with an evil gleam in his eye. In one hand he held a bell that had a most irritating clang, and in the other hand he held a wet sponge. As he moved down the room he paused at each bed, checking to see if the occupant was sleeping. There was nobody in the first bed, but as he whipped back the covers on the second bed, he laughed with glee as he exposed a cowering, disorientated boy.

"Wakey, wakey," he shouted, leaning down close to the boy's ear and squeezing the wet sponge over his head. The boy jumped up gasping, and wiped the cold water off his face.

Dean laughed and looked around the room to see if anyone else was amused. He spotted Peter at the end of the room, pointed a confident finger at him and slid the finger across his neck. "Dead," he mouthed, his lip turning up in an evil sneer.

Peter watched him uneasily. Who in their right mind could have thought that making Dean the class prefect was a good idea? He glanced around the dormitory to see if anyone could help him. He needed back up.

There was no point in asking Ronan for help. He was sitting on his bed, nervously watching Dean out of the corner of his eye. He might have been good for doing projects, but he was not good for standing up to bullies. The other boys in his room would be no help either. Normally he would have asked his best friend Olly, but Olly was a day pupil – he went home to his parents every night. He looked around the large room at the tall walls and long sash windows that loomed down on him. Feeling like a trapped rat, he desperately tried to think of a way of escaping.

Maybe he could run away – but they would surely catch him and then he would be in worse trouble.

He could pretend to be ill and go to the sick bay – but Mr Grimes would never believe he was sick. Or, he wouldn't care. Sick or not, Mr Grimes would shake him like a dog.

He could try to hide in the toilets – but that would be the first place they would look when they called the roll and found him absent from the class.

With each thought, Peter's face lit up with hope, but fell equally fast as each idea was dashed. There was no way, as far as he could see, that he could avoid getting into trouble. Every scenario he thought of, ended up with him in the principal's office. Billy and Dean would be so delighted at his misfortune; he could almost hear the sound of their horrible laughter as he was hauled all the way down the corridor to the principal's office by his ear.

He dressed himself in his navy uniform and carefully put his walkie talkie into his trouser's pocket. Olly had been given a pair of walkie talkies as a present from his parents, and he and Olly used them to send messages to each other. Then, looking around the peaceful dormitory one last time, he left the safety of his room and joined the crowded corridor of boys, who were making their way towards the canteen. A stale smell of yesterday's greasy dinner wafted up the winding stairs, making Peter's stomach feel worse. He wistfully thought how great it would be if he had an invisible power and could disappear for the day, escaping from all his worries.

But even though Peter wished desperately for some outside force to intervene, there was no sign that on that day his wish would come true. Nobody could have foretold why Peter, a normal, fun loving schoolboy, would be transformed so suddenly and so drastically. That Monday morning, there was no indication that something extraordinary was about to happen to him. Something that would change his world forever.

Chapter 2

Monday mornings were the worst day of the week. All the boys dreaded Monday. Not only was it the beginning of a very long week, but it always started with a triple class in English. A triple class with Mr Grimes! It was torture. Even Mr Grimes seemed to dread it. As the class dragged on and on, it seemed like the bell for break time would never ring. The boys yawned and squirmed in their seats. Now and again, a paper airplane flew across the room and a boy scampered like a little mouse across to the other side to retrieve it.

At the top of the classroom, behind his desk, sat Mr Grimes with his head propped precariously on his two hands and his eyes half-closed. A sound like a pig looking for truffles in a forest came snuffling from his hairy nostrils. From time to time his head would slip through his hands and he would jerk himself upright, giving a little shake and frowning from under his bushy eyebrows. And then slowly, in time to the tick of the classroom clock, his heavy head would slowly fall back into his hands.

Peter sat nervously in his seat beside Olly, looking warily around the room for any sign that Billy or Dean might be up to something. By turning his head very slightly to the right, he could see them out of the corner of his eye and still make it look like he was reading from his book.

"What's up?" whispered Olly, breaking through his thoughts. "You don't look too good."

"I'm in for it," replied Peter, under his breath. "I haven't done my project. He's going to kill me."

"Really, Peter? Why not?" said Olly. "You're going to be so dead. I have mine finished. Have a look at my cool plane!"

He picked up a beautifully painted, wooden airplane from the desk and turned it over, showing him the underneath. "It's got a motor that drives the propeller, and when you release these elastic bands, it shoots the peas straight out of the barrel here."

Olly clearly wasn't interested in Peter's problem. It wasn't fair. You could be sure that Olly's mother had spent hours on this project with him. "That's pretty cool all right," Peter whispered, enviously looking at Olly's happy and carefree face. "But what about me! What am I going to do?"

Just then a shadow fell over their desks. They looked up with apprehension to see Billy and Dean standing over two timid boys who were sitting in the row of desks behind them. The two boys looked up at Billy and Dean, and nervously scrunched up a note they had been writing.

"Beat it, losers," Dean growled, and he dumped them out of their chairs and down on to the ground.

The two boys scuttled to get out of Dean's way but in their haste, one of them tripped over his chair, sending it crashing into a table. The noise echoed around the quiet classroom. They froze, and there was a sudden silence as everyone glanced up at Mr Grimes to see if the noise had woken him.

It had.

"What was that?" barked Mr Grimes, jumping to his feet. The sound of his booming voice sent a shiver of fear down every boy. There was a quick scurrying as everyone dashed back to their seats, hurriedly looking down at their books to avoid Mr Grimes's gaze. He glared around the class, daring the boy who woke him to give himself away. Then, to Peter's horror, he heard Billy's voice from behind him.

"That was Peter, sir. He threw us out of our seat!"

"Sir … I didn't," Peter protested. "*They* threw the chair. They're trying to get me into trouble."

Billy looked up with an innocent expression on his face. "What ... us, sir? We haven't moved, sir."

Mr Grimes's face started to twitch. A red flush began to emerge from his shirt collar, rising quickly up his neck and spreading to both cheeks. This wasn't a good sign.

He glared at Billy. "You ... shut up!" he snapped. He then turned to Peter and spoke in a quieter but more deadly voice. "I am warning you, Peter. If you cause any more disturbances in this class, I will be extremely annoyed. And you don't want to see me getting annoyed now, do you?"

"No, sir. I don't, sir," stammered Peter.

"Because when I get annoyed, I have to think of a punishment, and the last time I had to do that, I don't remember it ending well."

He was right there. The last time Mr Grimes was creative with his punishments, he put a black mark high up on the wall and made a boy stand on his tippy toes for a whole hour, with his nose touching the mark. The boy had a crick in his neck for a week.

"So, I don't want to hear another word from you," continued Mr Grimes. "Now boys, open your books on page twenty-one and get back to work."

Peter turned around and scowled at Billy. He was met with a jeering smirk. "Got you into trouble," whispered Billy, in a sing-song voice.

Peter turned back to his desk in anger. He really wanted to get revenge. They were so annoying. His heart was pounding with rage, fear and embarrassment. But his thoughts of revenge were disturbed by the continuous whispering and jeering voices from behind him. *"Got you into trouble!"*

He pulled his chair in closer to the desk, wishing he could turn his chair around. Sitting with his back to them offered no protection.

Then suddenly, he felt something sharp prick him in his bum. It felt like he had received an injection with a very blunt needle. He jumped in his seat and looked around. Dean was covering his face with one hand to hide his laughter and in the other hand he held a compass which he had obviously used as a weapon. Peter pulled his chair in under the desk to get further away from them, rubbing his bruised bum tentatively. As he did so, he felt something wet and looked at his hand – a spot of blood had seeped through his trousers, onto his fingers.

He hissed at them under his breath. "Quit it ... that hurt!" His whisper came out louder than he intended, and he looked up in dismay to see the large bulk of Mr Grimes rising again from behind his desk.

"Peter! You again. I warned you!" came the thunderous voice. "Come up here. Now!"

Peter looked up in fear at Mr Grimes's two angry eyes which, like a chameleon, seemed to be looking at every boy in the class at the same time. Peter wondered what he actually saw out of those two crooked eyes.

"Sir!" he cried. "They stabbed me with a compass!"

"What are you talking about? Get up here now!" shouted Mr Grimes, pushing his chair back roughly and standing to his feet. He reached out on his desk, grabbed hold of a magazine and smacked it hard on the table. There was a loud crack, and everyone jumped. Peter dragged himself up to the front of the classroom and stood a few feet from Mr Grimes's dreaded desk.

"Come closer, boy," came the sinister voice from high above him. The magazine was still in Mr Grimes's hand, rolled up into a coil, and he tapped it menacingly into the palm of his other hand.

Peter gulped and took the tiniest step forward. Impatiently, Mr Grimes grabbed him roughly by the shoulders, his fingers digging into Peter's flesh.

"Look at me, you cheeky brat!" he snarled.

Peter raised his eyes from under his fringe while keeping his head down, trying to shield himself. He braced himself for the inevitable shaking.

And then it came – with more force than he imagined. The bony fingers gripped his shoulders and shook him like a crazed man with a cango drill. Peter's head flew back and forth. His teeth rattled and the world swam around him as he tried to keep his balance. From above, a vile stench of hot steamy breath wafted down to him. Mr Grimes drew his lips back in a grimace, revealing a row of teeth that seemed to be glued together with a brownish paste; teeth that hadn't seen a toothbrush for many years. Peter gulped, as he tried to hold his breath.

"I. Don't. Want. To. Hear. Another. Word. From. You! You are disrupting the whole class. Get your bag and go to the principal's office immediately!" As each word was spat out, the purple hairy face shook. With a final violent shove, he pushed Peter out the door. "Get out of here!" He slammed the door shut, and Peter was left alone.

The long corridor, normally crowded with students, was now empty and strangely quiet. All the students were in class. The principal's office was just down the corridor beside the entrance to the school. Peter stood there, not knowing what to do. He blinked as he fought back the sting of tears welling up in his eyes. Feeling very small and afraid, he picked up his schoolbag from the neat row of bags against the wall, and slowly dragged one foot after the other towards the principal's office.

Chapter 3

As Peter treaded to the looming office of the principal, he noticed that the door was open. He peeped through the window and saw an empty space behind the desk.

It looks like he isn't there, Peter thought. No – he definitely wasn't there. The room was empty. Phew! He was safe for the moment ... but the principal would be back. Peter stood there, rooted to the spot, not knowing what to do. He felt like a rabbit standing outside the den of a fox, foolishly waiting for the fox's return.

Then he noticed the school entrance and suddenly a thought crept into his head; he could just sneak out there while no one was looking and run away! He looked up and down the corridor, holding his breath. There wasn't a soul around; there was an almost eerie silence. The coast was clear.

Do it – do it now – run! a little voice in his head seemed to say to him. He walked towards the big door, his heart suddenly pounding in his chest. His hand faltered before it touched the cold steel handle. But with sudden determination he moved forward and pushed the heavy door open. It creaked slowly as it swung back and there it was; freedom – just in front of him. He stepped outside into the cool air and looked all around in trepidation.

The school rose up high on both sides and towered down above him. Row upon row of large dark windows, each reflecting the sky, loomed down on him like eerie shadowy figures. Somebody could be looking out of any of those windows and they would see him, but he had to keep going. It was too late to turn back. Releasing his grip on the handle, he forced one foot in front of the other, and started to walk down the driveway. He tried to hold his head high, and act like it was normal to be heading out of the school at this time, but the driveway seemed so long.

At last, he reached the big iron gates that formed the entrance to the school, and he walked out onto the road. A feeling of relief flooded over him. He had done it; he had escaped. He had tricked Mr Grimes! He couldn't wait to tell the boys. They would be so impressed.

But as he stood there looking around him at the cars passing to his left and right, his delight slowly faded. What was he going to do now? He couldn't go home – his parents be furious with him.

He could go into town, but it was quite far away. It was so far, he could only just make out the buildings that formed the skyline, tall and spiky. There was the familiar church steeple on the hill, and beside it, with the flat top, was the old tower. But to the left of the tower, his eye caught sight of some unusual bright lights moving round and round. He squinted at the flickering lights, trying to bring them into focus and after a minute, he was sure that what he was looking at was a ferris wheel, peeping above the top of the high buildings. The fair must have arrived! Imagine if he was to have a ride on the big wheel? The boys would be so jealous when he told them.

So, half-running and half-walking, Peter set off down the road, feeling both the thrill of excitement and pangs of nerves. Ducking off school was bad enough, but going into the town, which was forbidden under any circumstance, was going to end him in real trouble if he was found out. Every few minutes, he glanced over his shoulder, checking to see if the burly form of Mr Grimes was behind him. But there was no sign of anyone, and at last he reached the centre of the town, thirsty and out of breath.

He was completely unaware that it was in the market place where "*The Change*" would take place.

****

Peter stood on the footpath under the colourful canopies of the market stands, staring across at some baskets that were filled with sugary doughnuts.mj The smell of freshly baked cakes and melting chocolate was overpowering, as it wafted over to him. His stomach gurgled and a dull ache reminded him that he'd had no breakfast and he'd missed lunch. He was starving. He rummaged in his pockets, feeling for some money, but with exasperation he found that they were empty.

How am I going to buy food with no money? he thought, pulling his pockets inside out to be absolutely sure there were no coins hidden in the corners. *I'm not going to be able to survive until this evening.*

He gazed again at the doughnuts, his mouth watering in anticipation of the delicious sweet taste.

Maybe I could dash over when no one is looking and grab one, he thought. *If I'm very quick, no one will notice.*

Leaving his bag down on the ground, Peter waited until the fat man behind the counter was looking the other way, and then he cautiously crept forward. As he approached the stall, he ducked below the counter so that the side of the stall concealed him. Then he stretched his hand up over the counter and felt around for the pile of chocolate doughnuts.

He had it! The soft, sticky dough felt so good in his hand. He turned to run away, but just then he heard a roar from the man behind the counter. "Thief! Catch that boy!"

He jumped in panic and his heart sank in dread. He was going to get caught! He started to run, his feet barely touching the ground. To his horror, he felt an arm grab him on the shoulder, but he twisted away and dodged it. Sprinting as fast as he could, he ducked and darted between the crowds. The fat man followed him in hot pursuit.

He can certainly move when he wants to, Peter thought grimly. Looking over his shoulder, he could see that there were two men chasing him now. "Block him off!" they shouted. "Corner him!"

Up ahead, people jumped in front of him, trying to block his path. He sneaked under their arms, shot between their legs and twisted past them just as they tried to grab him. But his short legs were tiring. He couldn't keep this up for long. There were so many people trying to catch him; he couldn't see a way through them – he was going to get caught.

Right about now I could really do with a super power, he thought. *Oh, why could I not just turn invisible? Please, please make me invisible.* He squeezed his eyes shut, concentrating with all his might. *Pleeeassse! I'll do ANYTHING.*

And then the oddest thing happened.

Chapter 4

As Peter dodged a big guy who was blocking his way, he noticed that the man was not looking *at* him but seemed to be looking *through* him – at something behind him.

A shout started up. "Where's he gone, the little brat! Did anyone see where he went?"

The men stopped running and started looking around them. Peter desperately looked for somewhere to hide. Spotting a display table covered with a long tablecloth, he quickly ran over to it and crawled underneath. The table cloth hung down to the ground, concealing him completely. He exhaled slowly, looking fearfully at the white cloth walls that surrounded him. The shouting continued as the crowd became confused.

"He went this way," a lady called, and her voice became distant as she ran in the opposite direction.

"No, he didn't," cried another voice, deeper and closer. "Are you blind? He's in there under one of those tables."

"You go that side, and I'll go this side," called yet another voice. It sounded like there were people coming from every direction.

Suddenly, the tablecloth parted, and the sweaty bearded face of the doughnut man appeared just in front of him. Peter jumped in fright and held his breath, knowing that the game was up. He would be hauled out and handed over to the police. But the angry eyes looked straight through Peter as they searched under the table. Glancing around, the man swore and stormed off. What was going on? Why didn't the man catch him? He was right in front of him.

Then Peter got the shock of his life. The doughnut that he had taken, all sprinkled and chocolaty, was hovering in the air just in front of him. He could feel the doughnut in his hand and could see dents in it where his fingers had melted the icing, but there were no fingers to be seen. He looked down – there was absolutely nothing there; just the dirty ground below him. He shook his hand urgently. Where had his body gone? He felt like he was floating.

Panicking, Peter jumped up and promptly banged his head on the table. He crouched down again and listened to hear if anybody had heard the noise. He could still hear them, but their voices were distant.

"He's gone. He just disappeared," said a deep voice.

"That's weird. How could he just disappear? He must be here … we'd have seen him if he ran off," said another.

"Keep looking. I'm going to kill him when I find him," said a voice that sounded like the doughnut man.

Peter looked down again at his missing body and reached out to feel for his leg. He was relieved to feel that it was still there and felt quite normal. He quickly felt all the other parts of his body; head, chest and arms. Everything felt normal. But he couldn't *see* anything. What had he done to himself? Was he dead? Had he turned into a ghost? It didn't feel like he was dead. But then again, he wouldn't know what being dead would feel like. He felt totally normal.

The doughnut fell to the ground untouched as Peter's mind raced; he was in shock. So many questions were going through his head as the reality of the situation hit him. He thought of what his father was going to say to him. If he was in trouble before, he was *really* in trouble now. What had just happened? He went over the events of the past few minutes in his mind and remembered that he had made a wish. *Please make me invisible.*

Could it really be possible that his wish had come true and he actually *was* invisible? He couldn't see his hands, he couldn't see his feet. There was no sign of his tummy and he had to assume that his head was also invisible. Certainly, when he crossed his eyes, he couldn't see his nose.

And when he stuck out his tongue, he couldn't see that either. He pinched himself to make sure that he wasn't dead, and he definitely felt the pain. "I *am* invisible," he thought. "This is incredible!"

Peter felt the blood rushing through his veins as a mixture of fear and excitement started to build up inside him. *They can't catch me now!* he thought. He listened for a moment, but the sounds of the people outside had subsided to background chatter.

If nobody can see me, he thought, *then now is probably a good time to leave.* He looked around for his bag but there was no sign of it. Kneeling down, he patted the ground all around in the small area under the table cloth. There was nothing there; his bag was missing.

Drat it, he thought in exasperation, remembering that he had left it on a doorstep on the side of the street, just before he approached the stall. He had to get that bag. All his school books were in it – there was no way he could abandon it.

Cautiously, he parted the table cloth, wondering how long the invisibility would last. If he crawled out now, would be become visible again? But he couldn't stay there all day. He peeped his head out, keeping an eye on the position where his hand should be. If he saw his hand becoming visible again, he would dash back under cover.

All was good so far. Where his hand should have been, there was absolutely nothing to be seen. The table cloth moved, but no one was looking in his direction to see it. Edging slowly forward out from under the table, he made his way over to the line of stalls, slipped behind them, and crept down the street. Everything had calmed down again. Some men had resumed their positions, trying to attract customers to their stalls and calling loudly, "Oranges, five for a euro!" And at one corner of the market square, a man had a stick with a hole in it and was making the most enormous bubbles that floated gently down the street. All was peaceful.

Peter continued along the street slowly. As he moved, his hand kept dropping down to feel his tummy or his leg to reassure himself that they were still there and that this was not all just a dream.

"*I'm invisible!*" he said to himself over and over again in disbelief. "*I'm really invisible.*"

When he looked down at where his feet should have been, he felt dizzy and unbalanced – as if he was walking on a tight rope, high above the ground. He shook his head to concentrate on the task at hand.

Just up ahead he could see the doughnut stall. The fat man had resumed his position behind the counter. Peter scanned to the far side of the street where he thought he had left his bag. There it was! Sitting innocently on the step at the opposite side of the market beside two ladies who were chatting.

He crossed the square cautiously, being careful to go around people and not expect them to move out of his way. It would not do to bump into someone. The bag was nearly within reach. But just as he stepped forward to get it, one of the ladies – a particularly large lady – stepped leisurely sideways, blocking his path. He stood behind her, and patiently waited for her to move off. Ten slow minutes passed and still the ladies continued to talk.

"Did you see all the commotion here a few minutes ago?" said the large lady. "Some boy stole something and ran off. The police were here, and everyone was looking for him."

Is that me they're talking about? thought Peter. They'd certainly changed the story along the way.

"No, I missed that," replied her friend.

"Well they didn't get him," said the large lady. "So watch out for your handbag in case he's still around."

Peter couldn't wait any longer. Confident that there was enough room, he ducked down and held his breath, slowly stepping forward to creep past her. It was a tight squeeze. After just two steps, he froze, seeing her skirt move as he brushed against her. The lady looked down, passing her hand over her thigh, but there was nothing to see, so she stepped back, looking around with a puzzled expression.

Peter kept going, and without thinking, put his hand out to pick up his bag as he had done a hundred times before. The red bag that had been sitting quietly on the step, lifted into the air – the handles limp and drooping down. It hovered for a second as if thinking in which direction it would go, and then slowly moved off all by itself. Peter looked down and his heart jumped. He hadn't anticipated how strange it would look, but the shock on the woman's face said it all. Peter might have been invisible but the things he held were not. For an instant his eyes locked with the woman's surprised eyes. It seemed as if she was looking directly at him.

"Jenny! The bag – look at the bag!" she cried, clutching her friend's arm. "It's moving all by itself."

Peter turned away from her and ran, trying to avoid everyone in his path. The people stopped what they were doing and stared in amazement at the sight of the red bag floating past them mid-air. One lady tried to grab the bag but found out that it had a mind of its own as it slipped through her fingers and continued on.

Peter started to panic. He was attracting a lot of attention. Another hand reached out to grab the bag and held on to it tightly. Peter wrenched the bag free and ran down the street, heading for the nearest large shop. He reached an entrance and dived sideways off the street not noticing in front of him, a sliding glass door that was shut.

"Ow!" Peter let out a roar and banged straight into it. *The sensors don't detect me!* he thought, as he smashed his forehead off the door and his hand slammed against the glass. The bag was knocked from his hand and Peter fell to the ground.

Chapter 5

As Peter lay on the dusty ground, trying to gather his senses, the door suddenly slid open and a lady approached from inside the shop. Peter jumped up, abandoning the bag, and started to run past the lady. But his foot caught on the step and he stumbled, falling clumsily into the shop. There was a crash and he lay on the floor for a split second, looking around to see if anyone had noticed.

They had. The lady's jaw dropped as she stared, wide-eyed at the ground in front of her, desperately trying to see what her ears were hearing. Behind the counter, the shop owner strained to see what was causing all the commotion.

"Are you all right, madam?" he called out. "You look like you've seen a ghost. Did you hurt yourself?"

"Th-there's something there," whispered the lady, leaning against the wall to steady herself.

"Where?" asked the shop owner. He walked around the counter to her. "I don't see anything, but I did hear an awful bang. Did you hurt yourself?"

"Ssh," replied the lady. "Can't you hear that sound?"

By this time, Peter had scrambled to his feet and was scurrying down one of the aisles in the shop. With each frantic step, his runners squeaked on the polished floor.

"What the heck?" said the shopkeeper, as he stared down the aisle after the squeaking sound. "Did you see what went down there? It sounds like a rat."

"That's what I was talking about," said the lady. "Something crashed into the door and ran past me, but it was going so fast, I didn't catch sight of it. It wasn't a rat though – it was something much bigger."

"That's really weird," muttered the man under his breath. "Listen," he continued in a louder voice. "You stand there so it can't can get past you." He pointed with a flapping arm, indicating to the lady to go down the aisle next to the one that Peter was in. "I'll go down this aisle and we'll catch it."

The lady looked unsure but walked to the aisle and spread out her arms like she was herding some cows. The shopkeeper started to make his way down the aisle to where Peter was standing, hands outstretched like a blind person, feeling the space in front of him.

Peter was a little further down the aisle, frantically trying to think of what to do. The man couldn't *see* him, but he was going to *feel* him. He was getting closer. There was no room to squeeze past him and even if he did, the door was still closed.

The man was approaching slowly, staring blankly in front of him, searching to the left and right for anything unusual. Peter pressed himself up against a shelf of breakfast cereals hoping that the man would continue past him without feeling him. Suddenly there was a shout from over by the checkout. "There! On your right! Those boxes are moving."

A teenage boy, who had been watching the goings-on with curiosity, was pointing directly at Peter and was now running up the aisle behind the shopkeeper.

What's going on? thought Peter. *How can they see me? Is the invisibility wearing off?* But then, a box of cereal crashed to the ground from behind him and he realised he must have been causing them to move.

He ran to the back of the shop and looked with horror at the sight of the lady approaching him from the other aisle. *Oh no! They're coming at me from all angles!*

"What the heck?" cried the shopkeeper. "What's going on! What is it? I can't see anything. It must be a rat. Can you hear the squeaking? It's at the back there. Move up and corner it."

"I'm telling you, it's not a rat," said the lady. "But why can't we see it?"

The man moved faster, followed closely by the boy. The lady was also at the back of the shop now. There was a look of excitement and anticipation on all three faces as they searched wildly around, their eyes wide, like people in the darkness, searching blindly for something they couldn't see.

Just then Peter noticed another lady customer approaching the shop from outside. She hesitated at the door as she debated whether to enter the shop, or not. Peter willed her to come in. "Hurry up! Just let that door open!" he thought in desperation.

"It's over there!" cried the shopkeeper. "I can hear it panting!"

The shopkeeper lunged, making a grab where the sound was coming from. "Got it!" he said triumphantly, and Peter felt the strong arm of the man grab him around the waist. Peter twisted himself free, ducked and charged past the boy, shoving him violently out of his way. The boy was caught off guard; winded by the blow to the chest, and he fell over. Peter ran down the aisle and dashed over to the door. He could see freedom just on the other side of the glass – but the door remained resolutely shut.

The customer outside took another step towards the door, peering through the glass. *Come on, come on, come on!* Slowly, the door slid open.

"Stop that thing!" roared the shopkeeper to the entering customer.

"What thing?" she said, looking around in surprise and confusion.

The door was open! Peter darted past the lady and out to freedom. He ran down the street as fast as he could and when he was sure there was no one following him, he ducked into a disused doorway, leaning against it for support as he tried to get his breath back.

Wow! That was close! He was shaking. He was safe – but only for the moment; they had nearly got him. He was angry with himself for being so careless and thoughtless.

He cautiously looked down the street to the shop he had run from and noticed that a few people had gathered around in a circle. They were bending over, looking at something on the ground. It was his red bag! He had nearly forgotten it again. But it wasn't going to be easy to get. A man was picking up the bag in his hands and inspecting it. From the urgent look on his face and from his hand gestures, Peter guessed he was trying to convince the people that the bag was flying on its own, just a few minutes previously.

Peter could see from the expressions on the faces of the other people that they clearly thought that the man was mad. One by one, the people walked away and went back to their business. The man was left puzzled, turning the bag over in his hand again and again as he examined it. He looked around suspiciously, as if he expected more unusual things to happen. Peter almost felt sorry for him. But eventually the man turned and ambled back to his stall, still scrutinising the bag. Peter realised that, for the moment, he was going to have to abandon his bag.

****

Mr Grimes stood by the classroom window gazing thoughtfully at a point far away outside. In his hand he held a pen. The pen had a button on the top for clicking it on and off and his thumb rested on the button as if it was the trigger of a gun. Click, click, click. The noise echoed around the empty, silent classroom. His eyes were fixed on the distant view of the town. He could just about see the tip of the big wheel rising above the far away buildings with its colourful lights.

Where was the boy ...

Just after he had sent him out of the room to the principal's office that morning, Mr Grimes remembered that the principal was in a meeting and would not be back until the evening. But he had a class to teach so he didn't go to look for him. He assumed that Peter would return presently. So, the class continued in relative peace until the bell rang for lunch. All the boys trooped out for lunch but there was still no sign of Peter. Mr Grimes was not concerned then either – he was annoyed, but not concerned. The boy would turn up when he got hungry. They always did. He had been a teacher for a very long time and had yet to see one of them miss his dinner. Growing boys were always hungry.

But when the dinner gong rang, and then rang again to indicate that dinner was over, Mr Grimes began to feel a twinge of worry.

Where was the boy …

Peter had been behaving most oddly in the class that morning. As Mr Grimes stood there, remembering how the boy tried to make fun of him, his heart started to beat faster. His eyes narrowed, and he pursed his lips, so they disappeared and formed a severe line across his face. His thumb clicked faster on the pen. Peter was going to regret his disobedient behaviour. Mr Grimes would make sure of that. No one made a fool out of him. His breathing quickened as he planned a suitable punishment.

His gaze fell once again on the ferris wheel, far away in the distance. The lights were mesmerizing as they went around and around. And then his heart jumped. Of course! Why had he not thought of it before? He had heard the children talking with excitement that very morning about the arrival of the fair. Peter must have ducked off school and gone to the wheel. He was sure that he would find him there!

With new found enthusiasm, Mr Grimes jumped up to get his car keys. He was going to get that boy!

Chapter 6

Oblivious to Mr Grimes's determination to track him down, Peter made his way carefully down the street. There were still plenty of people around – some were idly looking in shop windows and others were briskly going about their business. Peter carefully gave each person a wide berth, looking ahead and planning his route down the street in advance. He was going to have to be much more careful. He needed to plan things instead of just rushing headlong. He was invisible, for goodness sake. How hard could this be?

He crossed the road, and around the corner his eye caught sight of the big ferris wheel in the fairground at the far end of the street. The wheel! He had completely forgotten about it. It towered above the buildings, the carriages glinting in the evening sun. He could see the people in the top carriages. They were pointing at all the different things they could see from high above the ground. The gentle breeze carried the sound of their carefree laughter all the way to where he stood in the street. *They don't have the problems that I have*, he thought glumly. Normally he would have loved to have a go on the wheel but at that moment, his heart wasn't in it. He had more worrying matters on his mind.

He stood there for quite some time, watching the wheel absent-mindedly, and wondering what to do about his tricky situation, when just across the road, he noticed a strange man with wiry, grey hair, looking around. He had his back to him, so Peter couldn't see him clearly, but the man looked suspiciously familiar. Where had he seen that hair before? He peered at him, wracking his brains. It couldn't be, could it? The man turned his head slightly to the right, revealing a set of bushy eyebrows and a purple face. There was no doubt. It was most definitely Mr Grimes! What was he doing there?

As if he had also spotted Peter, Mr Grimes turned around and started to stride purposefully towards him. In a panic, Peter headed briskly down the street looking over his shoulder to see if Mr Grimes was following. To his horror he saw that Mr Grimes was also marching down the street. But why? Had he come to town to search for him? And more importantly, did he have some way of seeing him?

The ferris wheel at the end of the street loomed closer and closer and suddenly a thought flashed through Peter's head. He could hide in one of the carriages! Mr Grimes would never think to look for him there.

"Laaast ride of the day!" called the man at the ferris wheel in a loud drawl. "Aaanyone else for the last ride of the day."

Mr Grimes's hulking form loomed closer. The sight of him approaching sprung Peter into action. He had to get on that wheel quickly. Peter slipped in behind the last two people in the queue, keeping as close to them as he dared. "Tickets please!" called the man to the couple. Peter watched his thick arm as it rested lazily along the length of the gate, controlling who could pass through. It didn't look like it was doing much, but Peter had seen how quickly it could spring to life should anyone dare to sneak past without paying.

The couple handed him their tickets, and just as Mr Grimes arrived, the gate opened to let them pass through. He was going to catch him if they didn't hurry up! Peter impatiently edged forward with the couple as they moved off. From behind their shoulder, he watched the terrifying form of Mr Grimes. His bony finger appeared just in front of him, tapping the man at the gate on the shoulder to get his attention.

"Did you see a boy in a blue school uniform here?" he shouted over the loud drone of the wheel's engine. Peter jumped in fear at the sound of his familiar angry tone.

The man shook his head briefly and turned to the couple. They slowly passed through the gate and Peter just scraped by with them as the man drew the gate closed behind him. He was in! The big wheel was just in front of him, looming up as though it could touch the sky.

The man motioned to Mr Grimes to wait as he brought the couple to their carriage. While he was busy putting the seat belts onto the couple, Peter slipped past and clamboured onto the carriage in front of them.

"I'm on!" he thought in relief as he settled back in his seat and waited impatiently for the wheel to move. He looked over to where Mr Grimes was standing. He was peering up at the carriages as if a sixth sense advised him that Peter was already on one of them.

A bell tinkled, and they were off! The wheel moved fast as it rose high up into the sky. He was nearly at the top. He gripped the sides of the carriage, a queasy feeling churning in his stomach. With the wind rocking the carriage, it didn't seem so stable now, and he wondered if this had been such a good idea after all. But then it started to descend, and he loosened his grip on the arm rest. Looking down, Peter could see the heads of all the people below. Mr Grimes was still waiting by the entrance gates, his wiry hair blowing in the wind. *What is he waiting for?* Peter thought with exasperation. *Why doesn't he go away?*

The wheel quickly swooped down and back up into the sky again. Around and around, up into the sky and down to the ground, until finally the bell tinkled, and the wheel stopped. The people in the carriage behind him got off the ride. Peter was glad it was over. It looked more fun than it actually was.

He looked down over the edge of the carriage to watch the people getting off. To his annoyance and discomfort, he noticed that Mr Grimes was *still* there, looking at the carriages as the people left.

And then his stomach gave a sickening lurch as he noticed a bigger problem. When the last carriage to be evacuated was at the bottom of the wheel, his carriage would be at the top. The wheel would probably stop in that position. He looked about with wild eyes as the wheel ambled around, pausing every minute to let passengers off. His carriage was climbing higher and higher.

He peered dizzily over the side of the carriage which was now high in the sky. The great steel bars formed a mesh beneath him, but the idea of swinging himself over the side of the carriage made him feel sick. There was no way he could do that. His knuckles were white from gripping the carriage and the more he thought about how he was going to get down, the tighter he clung to the bars.

He could see the man far, far down below, tidying up and preparing to leave. Mr Grimes was still questioning him.

A few minutes passed, and Peter waited, wondering what to do. It was cold on the wheel, high up in the sky. Dusk was falling, and the wind whipped around his jumper. The low drone of the wheel's engine slowed and then stopped, creating a silence in the evening. They were going to leave him there. *I have to stop them*, he thought. But if he shouted out, his cover would be blown.

Still the man below continued to sweep up, oblivious to Peter's turmoil.

He closed the gate and started to walk away. Mr Grimes fell into step beside him. Peter didn't care anymore. He was going to have to shout to them. They were not going to leave him behind. "Help!" he yelled. "I'm up on the big wheel."

Mr Grimes swung sharply around. "Did you hear that?" he said to the man. "That's the boy. I was right. He's here somewhere. I'd know his voice anywhere.

They looked up at the carriages in the evening light, checking to see if they could see anyone in any of them.

"There's nobody up there," the man said to Mr Grimes, turning around to leave. "I'm off home."

"Hey! Wait," said Mr Grimes, pulling at his coat. "I heard a cry. If there's someone stuck up there, you can't leave them up there all night!"

The man looked at Mr Grimes with irritation. "It's my dinner time. I want to go home."

"You need to turn back on that engine and check each carriage," said Mr Grimes with determination. "Or I'll have to report you to your boss."

The man sighed and turned back to the wheel, muttering under his breath, "Creepy weirdo!"

Peter looked down with relief at the sight of the man taking a big wad of keys out of his pocket as he entered the control room. But his relief was mixed with fear. He was going to have to get past Mr Grimes too, and Mr Grimes was sharp.

The silence of the evening was broken by the sound of the old engine cranking up. The big wheel creaked and started to turn slowly. Peter watched as the man and Mr Grimes checked each carriage carefully as they came towards them. Slowly Peter's carriage descended. He moved himself to the edge of the seat and prepared to jump. *One, two, three!* His feet hit the ground with a smack, and he fell over. Mr Grimes took a step forward, peering into the carriage. "Did you hear that noise?"

Peter didn't wait around. He scrambled up off the ground and ran off as fast as his legs could carry him. From the safety of the other side of the yard, he stopped, out of breath, and turned to see their reactions.

The man was looking around him warily as if the empty fairground was giving him the creeps. From the look on his face, Mr Grimes's presence was only adding to his discomfort.

But Mr Grimes was looking down the road to where Peter had run. His eyes narrowed with suspicion and Peter could just about hear the words he was saying. "There is something strange going on and I'm going to get to the bottom of it. I'm sure that the boy is behind it."

Chapter 7

Everything was going wrong for Peter. The feeling of being superman was fading fast and night time was approaching. What was he going to do now?

He was really hungry, and he needed somewhere to stay for the night. He couldn't go home. It was too far away and even if he did manage to get home, he would have to face his father and he couldn't do that. The last words his father had said to him as he dropped him off at the gate at the start of term were still fresh in his memory.

"If you misbehave at school this term, young man, you will be grounded for a week!" And Peter knew what that meant in his house. It meant being locked *outside* of the house, instead of locked inside. He shuddered at the thought. He didn't want to have to spend a week in the dark and cold, garden shed.

If he went back to school now, he would be in big trouble too. And how did Mr Grimes know where he was? Had he followed him? Had he seen what happened in the market? Did he know that he had become invisible? Peter was going to have to lay low for a while until he became visible again.

But in the meantime, what was he going to do?

He sat down on the kerb and watched the people as they cleared away the market stalls and packed up their vans for the evening. Everyone was going home for their dinner.

What would Olly do in this situation? He wished that he was there with him. A terrible feeling of loneliness and fear overcame him. If he was in school now, he would be having a nice warm dinner and playing with his friends. He sighed, wishing he had never left the school.

But then he remembered the walkie talkie! It was still in his pocket. He took it out and checked the time. It was 5.45. Olly would be at home now, so he could contact him. He hoped that Olly had the walkie talkie with him, and it was charged up. He pressed the "talk" button and to his relief, he heard the buzzing sound as it tried to make contact. Olly's walkie talkie was charged.

****

A few miles away, at number 10, Oakland's, Olly sat on the sofa, his homework books spread out in front of him on the coffee table. To the untrained eye, it looked like he was studying diligently, but on closer inspection, one could see that his pen lay idle on the maths sheet, and the pages of the book that sat on his lap had not been turned for quite a while. Olly's mind was on more important matters. Where was Peter? He hadn't turned up at lunchtime, and when he went to look for him in the dormitories, there was no sign of him there either.

A familiar buzzing sound coming from his school bag broke through his thoughts and he rummaged quickly around the bag trying to find his walkie talkie.

"Hello?... Hello?" came a crackly voice over the walkie talkie.

"Peter? Peter is that you! Where are you? Over."

"Oh, Olly, something really crazy has happened to me. I'm in town. I took a doughnut from one of the market stalls and then I turned invisible. Over."

"Hang on a sec," said Olly. "Be serious. Start from the beginning. What happened and where are you. Over."

"I *am* serious," replied Peter. "I'm invisible. I can't see any bit of myself at all. Over!"

"Peter, that's not possible. Stop joking. Where did you go and why didn't you come back to school? Over."

"I'm telling you. It's the truth. I left the school, went into town and I was starving. So, I took a doughnut from a market stall. I was going to pay for it later cause I didn't have any money. Then all these men started chasing me and calling me a thief! I just ran. But there were so many of them and they were catching up with me. So, I just wished that I could turn invisible to get away from them. You know, just like we always wish, and I hid under a table, and next thing I knew, I looked down at myself and there was nothing to see!"

Olly was silent for a moment as he tried to make sense of what Peter was saying.

"Over," said Peter. There was a pause and then he said. "Olly! Are you there?"

"Yeah, I'm here," replied Olly. "But even though this is a great story, I know it's not true. Over."

"Olly, please believe me! I swear to God it's true, and now I'm here on the street and I've nowhere to go. I can't go home, and I can't go back to school. I have to wait until this wears off and I'm back to normal. What am I going to do? Over."

"Well if you're invisible you can do anything," said Olly, still not believing him. "You can just walk into someone's house and spend the night there. You can go back to school and no one will be able to see you. You can go to the cinema and stay there all night. You can just go to the police station and tell them that you're invisible and they'll mind you. Over."

"Olly, I can't go to the police! Are you crazy? Someone might have reported me taking the doughnut. Over."

"Okay then, just go back to school. Over," said Olly calmly.

"But I can't do that. There are so many people there. If I bump into anyone, they'll tell Mr Grimes and he might tell my parents and then I'll be in even bigger trouble. They'll kill me if they see what I've done to myself. Over."

"Sounds to me like they won't be *seeing* what you've done to yourself," said Olly, with a smirk.

"Olly, you're not helping!"

"Sorry. Look, why don't I tell my mum to come and get you. Where are you exactly? Over."

"Olly, I can't tell anyone. If an adult finds out about me, they will definitely tell the police. They would have to. An invisible boy? It's never happened before. And what will the police do? They'll have to tell the government. They might think that aliens are involved, or another country has a chemical that can turn all their opponents invisible. They could do experiments on me to find out how this happened, and you know how I don't like injections! Over."

Peter's vivid imagination was obviously in overload with all the possible bad things that could happen to him.

"But Mum won't tell anyone. Over," said Olly.

"She might! You don't know what an adult would do. And also, I saw Mr Grimes at the ferris wheel. I think he was following me. I think he knows something's going on. Over."

"What are you talking about? Mr Grimes and a ferris wheel?" said Olly, getting tired of Peter's fantastical story. "Look, if you're not going to let Mum come and get you, then you're just going to have to find somewhere else to stay. Like an empty house. Then tomorrow I'm sure you'll be back to normal. It'll be fine. Over."

"Do you really think so?" asked Peter doubtfully. "Is that what you would do if you were me? You do believe me, don't you? Over."

"I don't know," replied Olly. "If I say that I believe you, I imagine I'll hear you roaring with laughter and telling everyone that I really believed that you had turned invisible. I'm afraid I'm going to have to see it to believe it. Over."

"It *is* true! How many times do I have to say it! Okay… I'll go. My battery is getting low. I'll contact you and let you know how I get on. If my battery runs out and I end up back in class, we can use our secret code to communicate. Over and out."

"Right so, Mr Invisible," said Olly, and he hung up.

Olly paused and looked at the walkie talkie in his hand. What was Peter up to? That was the strangest conversation he'd ever had with him. It didn't seem like Peter at all. Why would he make all that stuff up? Why wasn't he at school? He was right about one thing – he was going to be in big trouble if he carried on like this…

Chapter 8

Peter wasn't feeling any better. Olly's suggestions were no help at all. He'd mentioned going to the police, heading back to school, staying in someone's house or going to the cinema. Well, he wasn't going to go to the police, and he wasn't going to go back to school. He would have loved to go to the cinema, but it was miles away; it was definitely too far to walk. And his last suggestion was to stay in someone else's house. Did Olly really mean that? It was true that it would be unlikely that anyone would find him. If they happened to hear a noise that they couldn't see, they would be more scared of him then he would be of them. Certainly, in all the films he had seen, people were terrified if they thought there was a ghost in the house.

Maybe it *would* be possible to stay in a house, he thought. And if something bad happened to him, that would teach Olly a lesson. He'd be sorry for not believing him. And his parents would be sorry too, for being so mean to him.

He frowned, deep in thought as he went through all the possible outcomes in his head. He was going to plan it all properly this time, so there would be no chance of getting caught.

The first thing was which type of house to choose. It would have been a nice idea if he could have just chosen an empty house, like Olly suggested, where the people were away for the night, but that wasn't going to work. The front door would be locked if there was no one there and he couldn't get past a locked door. It was going to have to be a house with people inside. And then, he just had to make sure he was super quiet. If he didn't make a sound and he was invisible, no one would know that he was there.

So, feeling weak from hunger, he followed the road out of town, looking for a suitable house where he could get some food. After a while, he turned a corner and saw a group of houses in a row. A car was parked in front of one of them, suggesting that there was probably someone inside.

Peter pushed open the gate, tiptoed down the small garden path and looked inside the front window. A television was in the corner of the room, but there was no one on the sofa or in either of the armchairs beside the television. He decided to investigate the back of the house, and silently crept under an arch to the back garden.

A delicious smell of hot dinner lingered in the air at the back of the house, making Peter's mouth water. He breathed deeply, feeling like a hungry dog with a juicy bone being dangled in front of him. He paused at a window and peered inside. In the dim light he could just make out a sink across the other side of the room. Beside the sink, a pot sat on a cooker, the contents bubbling. He carefully looked around. Once again, the room was empty. Where was the owner of the house?

From nearby Peter could hear the sound of running water. He looked up and saw a steamed-up window. A pipe ran from the window to the ground and the sound was coming from the water gurgling in the pipe. *The owner must be upstairs,* Peter thought. *The coast is clear to make my entry.*

Oddly enough, Peter didn't feel very frightened at the thought of entering the house. For the first part of his plan, he was just going to nip in, get some food and leave. He could see the food in the kitchen; it was so close, and the hollow dull pain of hunger in his stomach made all other dangers fade into the background. The owner was obviously upstairs in the shower and Peter intended to be very quick. He'd be in and out in two minutes. This was a good plan. What could possibly go wrong?

41

He went over to the patio door and tried to slide it sideways. Fortunately, it slid open easily on well oiled runners and Peter slipped inside, leaving the door open behind him so that he could escape quickly if he needed to.

The kitchen was small and untidy. It looked like a robber had already visited it and had trashed the place looking for valuables. Dirty plates lay in the sink and on the counter top more plates and cups were strewn around haphazardly. Books and papers lay on the table and there was even a bundle of dirty clothes on the ground in a corner. But Peter looked around with satisfaction. A messy room was good – they wouldn't notice if anything was out of place.

The deep sound of a man singing above the low drone of a shower drifted down the stairs. Peter went over to the cooker. The scent of the dinner wafting from the bubbling pot was unbearable. Hunger gnawed in his stomach. He breathed deeply, his mouth watering, and looked for a bowl. But just then the sound of singing stopped. Peter paused and listened, his hand still on the bowl. He could still hear the thudding sounds as the person moved around upstairs. But he had to hurry up; the person could come down at any moment.

He was just about to ladle the dinner into the bowl and leave, when suddenly, without any warning, a large man appeared in the doorway wearing only a towel robe. He stood there motionless, blocking the exit. Peter stopped dead in his tracks. Forgetting he was invisible, he looked up at the man in horror, expecting him to show embarrassment at having been caught half naked, and shock at finding a strange boy in his kitchen. But the man just looked casually around the room as if he was missing something. Peter held his breath and squeezed his eyes half shut, praying that he would just go away! The man was so close to him. If he took just two more steps, he would be touching Peter.

"What did I come down here for?" the man muttered under his breath, looking vaguely around the room. It seemed to Peter that he was looking straight at him. He *must* sense that Peter was there – his heart was beating so loudly!

But then the man turned away, idly picking up a comb off the shelf. With relief, Peter watched him as he made to leave the room. He took two steps but then the man paused and frowned, staring intently ahead. Peter followed his gaze and his heart sank as he saw the open patio door.

The carefree expression left the man's face. He spun around, his eyes darting around the room suspiciously, looking for any sign of an intruder.

Peter flattened himself against the counter as the man strode purposefully towards him – one arm stretched out in front of him as if to grab something. Peter quickly stepped to one side to avoid him just as the arm reached for the drawer he had been leaning against.

Pulling open the drawer, the man took out a heavy, ceramic rolling pin. He closed the drawer and slowly left the room, gripping the handle of the rolling pin tightly.

Peter waited for a moment, and then tiptoed to the hall door that the man had passed through. He peeped around the door and watched the man as he slowly moved down the hall, checking behind the coat stand and in the small room under the stairs. Peter waited for a few minutes until he heard footsteps on the stairs and then he grabbed a bowl, filled it with the dinner and stepped out the patio door silently. He ran over to a bush and sat down behind it. Even though no one could see him, he just felt more comfortable not sitting in the open. He exhaled deeply and took a spoonful, relishing the delicious taste, as it warmed his hungry belly.

As the light started to fade, Peter began to feel the familiar fluttering of nerves in his stomach. It was time to execute the second part of his plan; to enter the house with no one hearing him, sneak upstairs without making a sound, and hopefully find a spare room where he could spend the night. This was going to be tricky. It was going to require all his super stealth tactics if he was going to pull this off, and the memory of the man holding the rolling pin in his hand did nothing to improve his confidence.

But just as Peter finished his dinner, he noticed something strange that distracted him from his plans – something he wouldn't have been aware of if he hadn't been invisible.

Initially, he didn't notice anything as put the empty dinner bowl down on the grass, but then, as he stood up to approach the house, he saw that half way between his head and the ground – where his belly should have been – there was a brownish, jelly like, floating mass of liquidy ... stuff. It was moving with him, as he moved. With growing curiosity, he put his hand out to touch it, but before he reached it, his hand collided with his invisible jumper.

Oh, my God! he thought. *That's my food digesting in my stomach! Oh, that is revolting.*

Peter was horrified. Had he really eaten that disgusting blob? Hovering in the air, it reminded him of the time he had been sick all over the bathroom floor and he had watched his mother as she cleaned up his vomit – all slimy and gloopy. The thought of it made Peter retch. He was thankful that his jumper had saved him from getting smelly puke all over his hand.

He stopped in his tracks and retreated to the bush. It wasn't going to be possible to enter the house at that moment with this mess in full view. He would have to wait until it was completely dark or until his food was digested. He sat down again and waited, watching as the light faded. He hoped it wouldn't be long before it was dark because his clothes were getting damp as the evening dew started to fall. After a while, the stars started to appear, shining brightly against the dark sky, and the moon peeped over the roof of the house, casting shadows in the garden. The temperature dropped, and he tried to pull his jumper tighter around him. But it was no good – he wasn't dressed for staying outdoors at night.

At what time will it be safe to enter the house? he thought. It was too risky while everyone was moving around. But he would have to enter soon. His fingers and toes were so cold he could barely feel them.

And then he remembered with fear, a story that his father had told him once about the war.

"Did you know, Peter," he had said, lowering his newspaper at the breakfast table, "that during the war, when the soldiers got really cold from living outside in winter, they got a disease called frostbite."

"What's frostbite, Dad?"

"Frostbite is a disease that you get if your body gets really cold," he repeated, with a slight smirk. "And your fingers and toes get so cold you can't feel them and then they freeze. Soon, they turn black – all the way from the tips to where they join the hand – completely black. They're rotten, you see. And after a period of time, the fingers and toes fall off."

"You're joking, Dad."

"I'm not joking, Peter. And if the men are found when the toes are black but haven't yet fallen off, they have to be cut off with a knife by the doctor."

"No!"

"It's true, Peter," he said, and he went back to his paper with a lingering smile on his lips at the look of shock on Peter's face ...

Peter glanced down at where his numb, stiff fingers should have been. His father had not mentioned the timescale. How long did it take for them to turn black and fall off? For all he knew, they could already be black, and they could fall off any minute! He had no choice. He had to get inside the house.

So, plucking up his courage he sneaked cautiously around to the front of the house and peeped in the sitting room window. The family were sitting on the couch munching popcorn from two big bowls and watching the TV. All was peaceful. It was time to make his move.

Chapter 9

All would have gone smoothly if it hadn't been for the toilet - the loud noisy toilet. The most annoying thing was that Peter had said to himself before entering the bathroom. *Don't forget to not flush the toilet.*

Initially the plan had gone relatively well. Peter had slipped inside the house without a problem. A welcome blast of warm air greeted him, and he paused with his hand still on the door handle, waiting to see if anyone had heard him. But there were no raised voices and he could hear "The Simpsons" playing on the TV. He looked around. He was standing in a hallway. Just in front of him was the stairs, leading to some rooms above. At the bottom of the hallway was the door to the sitting room. It was open, and the sound of their laughter drifted out.

Cautiously, he tiptoed over to the carpeted stairs and padded up. But half way up, there was a loud creak! Peter froze and lifted his foot up quickly. The step creaked again with the release of his weight. *Drat it!* From where Peter was standing on the stairs, he could see straight into the sitting room through the open door. He held his breath, his eyes fixed on the father, while he waited to see if they had heard him.

"What was that noise?" said the father, looking up sharply – directly at Peter it seemed – but then, thankfully, he turned his head and went back to watching the film. "Must be a creaky water pipe," he muttered, shovelling a handful of popcorn into his mouth.

Peter breathed a sigh of relief. He continued up the stairs testing each step cautiously with his hand before putting his weight on it. One slow step at a time and he made it to the top without any more incidents.

When he reached the top of the stairs, he quickly peeped his head around the door of each room and looked inside. Clothes and shoes were strewn all over place. But one room was empty except for a small unmade bed and a lot of dusty boxes piled high against the wall. Judging by the thick layer of dust, nobody had been in this room for quite some time. He looked around with satisfaction thinking that he could stay there for a while in peace. To the left, another doorway lead to the bathroom. A sudden urge came over Peter and he went inside and sat down on the toilet.

Don't forget ... do not flush the toilet, he reminded himself. There was a loud splash but there was nothing to see in the bowl when he turned to look. This one was invisible...

It was at this point that Peter's hand shot out automatically and pushed the handle on the toilet. Immediately, he tried to pull it back up again, but it was too late. Tssshhh! The sound of the toilet flushing echoed around the room, drowning out the noise of the TV downstairs. He had never noticed how loud the flush was on a toilet before, but once that handle was pulled, there was no going back. The water churned round and round for what seemed like an eternity and then the cistern filled up, like a thunderous waterfall.

In a panic, Peter ran out and scuttled under the bed in the spare room. A deep voice boomed up the stairs. "What was that noise? Turn down on the TV. I heard something upstairs."

There was a silence in the house as everyone strained to hear the sound. Peter could hear a sound all right - the sound of the water filling in the cistern. He didn't know if they could hear it from downstairs. But then his heart fell as he heard the heavy tread of the father's footsteps climbing up the stairs. He went into the bathroom, and from under the bed, Peter watched as the man paused in the doorway, listening with concern to the sounds from the toilet and watching the swirling water. He looked around with wide eyes to his wife who had appeared beside him in the doorway.

"There's someone in the house," he whispered in a low voice. "It could be dangerous. Go downstairs and stay with the girls. Don't say anything to them." The man stepped into the bathroom and then appeared after a moment with a large scissors in one hand, gripping it tightly and stabbing the air as if he was practicing attacking the intruder. Peter looked on in horror. The man wiped the sweat off his brow and left the bathroom, cautiously stepping into the girl's room. After a few minutes, he appeared again and moved into the next room, checking it slowly.

Peter's heart was beating fast. His breathing seemed so loud in the silence of the room. He held his breath, sure that the man was going to hear him when he returned, but then after a moment he felt like he was going to burst; he had to let go and that was even noisier. Any moment the man would come and check the room. Peter squeezed his eyes shut, praying that the man would pass by his room, but he had no such luck. With a sudden stomp, Peter saw the man's heavy feet standing at the doorway.

"He has to be in here," the man growled, and he stepped inside.

Although he was invisible, Peter realised that there was a small part of him that was *not* invisible. There was a chance that the man would notice the dark sludge in his tummy.

From his position under the bed, he could see only the big feet of the man, as they moved around the room and the sound of his laboured breathing filled the silence, drowning out any sound from Peter. He felt like Jack in the Beanstalk, hiding in the house of the giant. Peter watched with apprehension as the man checked the wardrobe and walked around the far side of the bed. Any moment now and he would check under the bed.

Sure enough, a pair of large knees came into view as the man knelt down, and then suddenly a big angry face appeared with a pair of scissors. But just as quickly as it appeared, the face disappeared, and the man left the room.

Peter exhaled slowly, listening to the footsteps dying away as the man went downstairs. Peter knew he had to get out of there; it wasn't safe. He would stay there quietly under the bed and leave first thing in the morning.

He waited for a few moments until he was sure that all was quiet and then he crawled out from under the bed and looked around for a pillow and a blanket, so he could settle down for the night. Everywhere he looked, there were boxes of toys and boxes with clothes spilling out of them. Behind one of the boxes, sitting up against the wall, there was a large teddy. Peter removed the teddy and put it under the bed. That would do for a pillow. There was no blanket in the room, but he found a large coat and crept under the bed pulling the coat around him. Slowly, he started to relax.

He lay under the bed for some time listening to the sounds of the family. After a while, they started making preparations for bedtime. There were loud protestations from the girls.

"Just five minutes more?" said one voice.

"After this game?" begged the other.

"Two minutes then, "came the voice of the mother. "And then brush your teeth, girls, and get into bed."

Heavy feet stomped up the stairs and Peter heard the deep breathing of the father as he briefly checked again that there was no intruder in any of the rooms. His head appeared around the door of Peter's room and luckily, he didn't seem to notice that the teddy was not in the same position.

Finally, they were all in bed and the mother started to read a story about Superman. Peter listened to the story and in a few minutes, he had nodded off to sleep, happily dreaming of flying through the air.

****

Unknown to Peter, down at the police station, the local police man, Sargeant Coppers, had been receiving some very strange reports all day from a number of concerned citizens.

At one o'clock, a very large man turned up at the cop station complaining that a boy from the local school had stolen a doughnut from his stand at the market. He said that even though he was annoyed with the boy, that was not the reason why he was reporting the incident. Something very odd happened after that.

"I chased the little brat and a few of the other guys helped, because I get out of breath very quick," he said. "And we nearly had him, but the little rat hid under one of the tables. And here comes the weird thing. When we looked under the tables, he was gone."

"There was no sign of him?"

"No sign at all. He just vanished into thin air."

"Okay," said Sargeant Coppers. "Just so I get this straight. You're not reporting a theft? But you are reporting a case of a vanishing boy."

"That is correct, sir."

"That's a most unusual statement. I'm sure that the boy is just very good at hide and seek."

"I would appreciate if you would take me seriously, sir," said the fat man. "The boy just disappeared."

"Ok ... I'll check it out. Thank you and good day," said Sargeant Coppers, eager to get rid of the man.

Then, just half an hour later, the phone rang, and a woman called, raving about a red school bag flying down the street by itself. This could possibly be explained. It was probably some boys playing a joke with a red kite that looked like a bag. But the woman also mentioned bumping into something solid beside the bag. Something alive that she could hear but not see. That was very odd, but there were plenty of mad people out there. Sargeant Coppers put it down to her being a crazy woman.

But later in the day, a man called into the police station reporting a similar story. He said that he had grabbed a flying bag, and also, that he had grabbed a coat, or something – it seemed to him to feel like a child –

but he couldn't see either the coat or the child. He heard it cry "ow" as it fell when he grabbed it.

Sargeant Coppers wrote all the details down in a notebook solemnly.

"So, it was a crowded street, yes? You're absolutely sure that the sound 'ow' didn't come from another person that was close to you?"

"Definitely not."

"How many other people witnessed this incident?"

"There were lots of people around. We were all talking about it."

"And what happened next?" said Sargeant Coppers.

"It escaped."

"You didn't run after it?" asked Sargeant Coppers. "Oh yes … I forgot. You couldn't see it in the first place."

"That's right."

"Hmmm. Okay, we'll handle it from here. Thank you for calling in." Sargeant Coppers snapped his book shut and started to walk back to his desk.

"Hang on a sec, I have the bag here," the man called.

"Really?" said Sargeant Coppers, turning around sharply. "Let's take a look at it then."

The man picked up a red bag off the ground and placed it on the counter.

Sargeant Coppers, remembering the story the lady on the phone had reported, examined the red bag carefully. But he could see nothing unusual about the bag – no mechanism that would enable it to fly through the air. He unzipped it and rummaged around inside, pulling out a few copy books and a pencil case. Then he noticed the name on the front of the copy book.

Peter Connor, 6th Class.

"Hmmm," he said, turning the bag over in his hands. "This doesn't look like anything special. Who is Peter Connor?"

"I suppose a child must have lost it. But I'm telling you, this bag was flying on its own."

Well, how about I hold on to it here, and when the owner calls to collect it, I'll question them."

"Well, okay then," said the man and he reluctantly left the station.

Sargeant Coppers scratched his head. What was going on? A second deluded person? Or was there a really clever trickster out there?

At 4.00pm, yet another man entered the police station. He said that he thought that his place of work was possibly haunted.

"And where do you work," asked Sargeant Coppers, thinking to himself. *Another nutbag? Have they all escaped from the asylum?*

"I operate the Big Wheel down by the market place," said the man.

"And what makes you believe that the Big Wheel is haunted? Is it starting up by itself?" Sargeant Coppers tried to keep a straight face.

"It isn't so much the Big Wheel itself – it's just that there were voices in the carriages, and they were moving all by themselves," said the man. "And there was this creepy man there, who looked totally crazy with wispy hair all over the place."

"And you're sure that there wasn't someone hiding in one of the carriages? Maybe trying to get a free spin?"

"No, we very carefully checked all the carriages."

"Do you think that the creepy man had something to do with it?" asked Sargeant Coppers.

"He might have. He was certainly very interested in what was going on… he wouldn't leave me alone."

"All right, all right," sighed Sargeant Coppers. "I'm sure it was just some boys having fun. But we'll look into it." He was getting tired of these trivial stories. What had happened to the days when he was in charge of high-speed car chases, looking for robbers?

At 5.00 pm, the Sargeant received a phone call to say that an eleven-year-old boy had been missing from the local boarding school, St Albans, since approximately twelve o'clock that day. They had searched the whole school and there was no sign of him. His school bag was also missing but all of his other belongings were still at the school. He had been told to go to the principal's office for misbehaving, but he hadn't appeared there. That was the last time he had been seen.

A missing boy in a St. Albans uniform? He quickly riffled through his notes from the morning. That was the school uniform the fat man said the boy who stole his doughnut was wearing. So … he wasn't a crazy man after all. The boy must have ducked off school.

"He left with a school bag, you say, Principal Stafford?" said Sargeant Coppers, suddenly pricking up his ears. "Was the bag by any chance red in colour?"

"Why yes, I think it *was* a red bag. Why?"

"And is his name Peter Connor?" asked Sargeant Coppers.

"It is. How did you know? Did you find him?"

"I have his school bag here. Someone handed it in. He's been up to mischief. The bag was found in town." Sargeant Coppers decided not to mention the reports of the bag flying by itself. He didn't want anyone accusing him of believing foolish stories.

"He went to town?" continued the voice at the other end of the phone. "I'll give him a piece of my mind when we find him. But in the meantime, we need your help. We don't want to have to call his parents. It would be most embarrassing to have to tell them that we've lost their son. It is most urgent that we find him."

"We will assemble a search party, Principal Stafford, and meet you at the school in one hour," said Sargeant Coppers.

****

By seven o'clock there were police men swarming around the school with their blue and white cars parked haphazardly and siren's flashing.

The boys in Peter's class were questioned but they had no useful information. One boy – Peter's best friend apparently – said that Peter had been very worried about his project, but he hadn't seen him since he disappeared. But as the boy spoke, he looked down at his feet and his ears went an alarming shade of pink.

He knows something, Sargeant Coppers thought. *I'll question him again later, when everybody has gone.*

With no sign of Peter in the school or on the school grounds, the detectives started house to house interviews. Nobody had seen a boy that matched Peter's photo. More people joined the search. They knocked on every house door; they searched every abandoned shed; they asked in all the shops, but except for the fat doughnut man, nobody had seen the boy. At 11.00pm that night, they called off the search and Sargeant Coppers reluctantly made the decision to call to Peter's parents.

After five minutes of dialing the number, an angry voice eventually barked down the phone, making Sargeant Coppers jump. "Who do you think you are, bothering me in the middle of the night?"

"Is this Mr Connor? My name is Sargeant Coppers. I'm calling from the police station at Woodlands Village, where your son goes to school."

"Oh, I beg your pardon, sir," came a more conciliatory tone. "Yes, this is Mr Connor. How can I help you?"

"I'm very sorry to disturb you, but your son is missing."

"He's what? Gone missing?" asked the father. "How can he go missing? He must be hiding in the school somewhere. I'll give him some thrashing when he's found. Ahem … I mean, I'll be very glad when he's found. We love our little boy very much. Is there anything we can do to help?"

"Yes," said Sargeant Coppers. "You can join the search!"

"Em," said the father, and there was a pause as if he was trying to think of an excuse. "Well, we're actually very busy at the moment and the school is quite far away. Maybe it's best if you handle this and let us know when he's found."

The police man put the phone down, thinking how odd it was that the father was not concerned. Maybe they were involved in the boy's disappearance. He would question them tomorrow. He set off home for bed, tired after the long day. *At least there were no more reports of invisible forces,* he thought. He scratched his head absent mindedly. *Hmmm … reports of an invisible force, possibly supernatural, and also reports of a missing boy whose bag was flying all by itself… all in a small town on the same day… Could they possibly be related?* It was all very strange. But he quickly forgot about it as his head hit the pillow and he was snoring within seconds.

Chapter 10

Not far away, at the man's house, Peter was also fast asleep, but not snoring, and not quite as comfortable, as he lay on the hard floor, under the bed. The night passed without incident and in the morning, an alarm clock woke him with a start. He jumped up thinking he was in the dormitory. His head hit the underneath of the bed and he fell back onto the teddy. Where was he? Why was he under a bed? Whose bed was it? Slowly he remembered the activities from the day before.

He looked down at his body. Was he still invisible? Yes, he most certainly was. He wasn't sure if he was happy that he was still invisible, or disappointed. A mixture of both emotions overcame him. Even though it was exciting that he was invisible, it was also a bit scary. He was still in a stranger's house, hiding under a bed and he still had to face going back to school, or telling his parents.

The sound of the father getting up and stomping around his room reminded Peter that he urgently had to leave this house. Hopefully they would all leave after breakfast and he could make his getaway unnoticed.

The family trooped downstairs and delicious smells of buttery toast wafted up the stairs reminding Peter how hungry he was. He listened to the general chaos as everybody got ready for the day; missing shoes, missing lunchboxes, dirty uniforms, homework not finished. It seemed like they would never be ready. But finally, the front door slammed, and the house was silent.

Peter jumped out from under the bed and ran to the window. The car was pulling out of the driveway and all four members of the family were inside. He was home alone for a whole day!

He dashed downstairs, not caring about making noise now. He went into the kitchen and made himself some toast and a cup of tea, humming a tune as he spread the butter and marmalade on the toast. Then he put it on a plate and went into the sitting room.

Turning the TV on to the cartoon channel, he sat on the couch, eating his breakfast and thought. *This is the life! Everyone else is at school, doing work, getting into trouble, and I'm sitting down to a day of TV and if I'm lucky I might find a PlayStation.* But as he flicked from channel to channel, he suddenly froze. There looking back at him on the TV screen, was a large photo of his face.

"MISSING BOY" was the title under the photo. Peter moved closer to the TV to get a better look.

"An eleven-year-old boy went missing from school at 12.00pm yesterday," the reporter said into the microphone. The camera panned out to reveal his teacher, Mr Grimes, standing to the left of the reporter, his wiry hair flying across his face in the wind.

"Peter was in class at twelve o'clock yesterday," Mr Grimes said. "And he was behaving quite oddly. I sent him out of the class because he was disrupting the other pupils. He was supposed to go to the principal's office. But he didn't go there, and he didn't return to the classroom."

The camera went back to the reporter. "There have been no sightings of Peter since then. Peter was well liked by his fellow classmates and his parents are very worried. Please contact the nearest police station if you have any news regarding this boy."

Then his mother's face came onto the screen, looking pale and older than he remembered.

"Peter, we love you very much. If you are out there, please come home." She looked very worried. His father also appeared and put his arm around his mother. Peter felt a lump in his throat. He missed his mother. Maybe he could go home? But then he remembered that she was not really very nice. Despite what she said on the camera, she normally

...1 t stand him being around more for than a day or two. And also, there was his father to deal with ...

Then, to his horror, onto the screen came Billy and Dean. "We were best friends with Peter. We really miss him, and we are so worried about him. Peter, if you're watching this, remember that we are waiting for you to come back."

They smiled at the camera, a simpering – I'm *such* a nice boy – smile. But Peter could see behind their fake smiles, the faces that really said. "We're waiting for you to come back... *to get you...*"

Peter's face felt suddenly very hot. He was boiling with rage. Just the sight of them made him so angry. He was going to get his own back on them. This time it might actually be possible with this new power. Billy and Dean would never tease him again. He frowned, deep in thought, as he began to plot his plan of revenge. There were a lot of things that he could do now that he was invisible, but he must ensure nobody would know it was him.

Finally, he had it all worked out. He was going to go back to the school, and he was going to teach those bullies a lesson. Every detail was clear in his mind. He could even picture the look of surprise and fear on their faces, and this thought made him smile. "Ha ha! I have the advantage now!" He was going to make good use of his superpowers. He just needed to pop into the joke shop on his way back to school to get the implements he needed for his plan – a permanent marker, a very sharp pencil, some itching powder and a stink bomb!

It took Peter an hour to walk back to the school, but at last he entered the tall iron gates again. As he walked down the long driveway, he looked in dread at the dark school as it loomed up in front of him, glowering under an air of menace. *But*, he reminded himself. *This time is different. I'm invisible. I'll just pop in, cause havoc and leave.*

When he finally arrived, everyone was back in class after lunch. He went around the back of the school and stood on his tippytoes, peeping in the window of his classroom. The teacher had not arrived yet and all the boys were talking and jumping around. He looked in the scrubby grass for a large stone to raise himself up and then took the first of the props out of his pocket – the permanent marker. Carefully, in big letters he wrote on the window. He had to write it as a mirror image so that the boys on the other side could read it correctly. He finished writing the message and waited for someone to look out the window but, to his disappointment, nobody looked around – they were far too busy chatting.

After a while the teacher came into the room. Everybody stood up to greet him.

"Good morning, Mr Grimes," they chanted together.

Mr Grimes did not answer. He wasn't looking at them. His eyes were fixed on the window, and he squinted and frowned as if he was trying to make out what was written.

"What is that on the window?" he suddenly roared.

Everyone jumped at the unexpected rage and they turned around to see what could have caused such an outburst.

"DEAN RULES," was written in big black letters on the top window, and

"MR GRIMES IS AN IDIOT," was on the bottom window. Mr Grimes's purple face started to shake. His whole body started to shake. Peter watched with delight from outside.

"Dean Morrissey! Get. Up. Here. Now!" shouted Mr Grimes.

Dean stared at the window and his mouth dropped in horror. He looked over at Billy, but Billy was doubled up laughing. The other boys were laughing too which made the teacher even angrier. Mr Grimes's eyes were fixed on Dean as a cat fixes it's eyes on its prey before pouncing on it.

 Reluctantly, Dean got up off his chair and walked to the front of the class.

"Dean Morrissey," said Mr Grimes. "You will spend the rest of the class in the corner. At lunch time, you will clean that window and after school you will stay back and write one hundred times, 'I will not write on school   windows'."

"But sir! It wasn't me!" protested Dean, looking around desperately.

"Your name is clearly written on the window," replied Mr Grimes. "How stupid can you be? Now, not another word, unless you want double detention!"

Dean went and stood in the corner, looking at the writing on the window with disbelief. Outside the window, Peter chuckled. He would come back later to watch Dean trying to clean the permanent marker off the window. Ha! He would be scrubbing for quite some time.

Now his attention turned to Billy. He hated Billy even more than he hated Dean. Sneaking around to the back entrance of the school he slipped inside and walked quietly down the empty corridors. But when he reached his classroom, he found, to his annoyance, that the door was closed.

He sat down, thought for a minute and came up with a plan of how to get into the room without anyone seeing the door opening on its own. Taking the permanent marker out of his pocket, he rapped loudly on the door and watched as Mr Grimes approached. The door opened, and Mr Grimes stepped out, looking up and down the empty corridor. "Hello?" he called loudly. "Is anyone there?" He waited for a moment muttering under his breath, and then turned to go back into the classroom.

But just as he turned, Peter threw the marker as far as he could down the corridor, in the other direction. It landed with a bang and rolled a few feet further before coming to a halt. The teacher looked around sharply at the sound and went down the corridor to investigate further. Peter caught the door as it started to close and slipped into the classroom.

That was nicely done, if I say so myself! he thought with a grin.

Chapter 11

Peter entered the classroom and looked around for Olly. He found him sitting in the front row and waved at him, but of course Olly couldn't see him.

It was a pity Olly was in the front row – Billy was in the back row and that was where all the fun was going to happen.

Creeping quietly down to the back off the class, Peter leaned over to Billy's ear. "Your turn, loser," he whispered. Billy looked over in surprise. But there was nobody there. The other boys had their backs to him, and their heads were lowered as they studied their books.

Just then Mr Grimes came back into the classroom and all the boys stood up to greet him. "Sit down, boys," he said. But as Billy went to sit down, Peter pulled the chair quickly from under him so that he landed with a bang on his bum on the floor. The whole class broke out in laughter.

"Silence!" shouted the teacher. "What is the matter with you all? You're irritating me greatly today! And will you sit down on your chair, Billy, or you'll be next in the corner up here!"

Billy pulled up his chair and sat down, red faced, looking around and glaring. Peter laughed to himself as he watched Billy trying to figure out who the guilty culprit was. The class continued in relative peace for a few minutes as the teacher's voice started his dull monologue again.

Time for my next trick, thought Peter. He felt in his pocket for the sharpened pencil and slipped it out. He leaned forward and stuck it nice and hard into Billy's bum.

"Ow!" Billy yelled, and he jumped up off his chair. "What's going on? Who did that!" He looked behind him but there was nobody there.

"Billllllyyyy!" Mr Grimes bellowed, causing the tables to vibrate. "Stand up!"

Billy did as he was told. Peter had never seen him look so frightened.

"What do you think you are doing disrupting the class continuously?"

Billy opened his mouth as if to reply, but from behind him Peter cut in, copying Billy's voice as best he could. "Stop shouting, sir. I can hear you perfectly well."

Billy wheeled around, a look of horror on his face.

Mr Grimes's jaw dropped. He stood in front of the class, opening and shutting his mouth, but no words came out. The class was now completely silent, enthralled by Billy's bizarre behaviour. All the heads turned at the same time from Billy to the teacher and back to Billy again.

Mr Grimes found his voice at last. "You cheeky young pup. How dare you!" Little bits of spit showered from his mouth and settled on the desk in front of him. "Never in all my years teaching have I heard such cheek!"

"But…" faltered Billy before Peter interrupted, drowning him out. "Sir, calm down. You are still shouting."

Everybody in the class was now staring agog at Billy, who was behaving as if he had completely lost his mind. Billy turned around again. He was now white with fear. Peter could barely stop himself from laughing as he tried to guess what Billy was making of it all. He was going to be in so much trouble.

"Get up here now," Mr Grimes bellowed, his voice shaking with rage. Billy scrambled up to the top of the classroom and stood in front of the teacher. Peter sneaked along behind him.

Mr Grimes grabbed Billy by the shoulders and looked down at him from a height. "Get into that corner and shut your trap," he bellowed, shoving him violently to the other corner of the room. "And face the wall!" he barked after him.

Billy ran over to the corner and looked relieved that that seemed to be the end of it. He looked over at Dean who was in the other corner.

"Ha ha!" mouthed Dean back to him. He was obviously in Dean's bad books too.

Peter was really beginning to enjoy himself – everything was going to plan. He only wished that Olly knew it was him that was causing all the trouble. He waited for a few minutes for the class to settle down again. Everyone was now on their best behaviour for fear of further upsetting Mr Grimes.

The next part of the plan was about to begin. Peter went up behind Billy, sprinkled some itching powder on Billy's pants and stepped away, waiting for the fun to start.

He didn't have long to wait. Within minutes, he saw Billy begin to twitch and shift his weight from one foot to the other. After a moment, he turned his head, quickly glancing around the class as his hand crept behind him, furtively scratching his butt. This initial scratch must have spread the powder onto his skin because, two seconds later, Billy was furiously scratching himself. He didn't seem to care any more who was looking at him – he was tearing himself apart.

Peter desperately tried to stifle his laughter; he could see that some of the other boys were in the same position as they stared at Billy. What had started as a furtive quick scratch was now a demented arse attack. He scratched his left butt cheek, rubbing it until he must have rubbed a layer of skin off and then he attacked his right butt cheek ... then back to the left, then both at the same time. His butt cheeks were hopping like they were alive! The itch must have been far worse than the embarrassment.

After a few moments, Mr Grimes began to notice that something was distracting the boys. Nobody was listening to him. He abruptly stopped talking and his eyes narrowed as he looked at the faces in front of him. In the last two minutes, their faces had changed from amusement as they tried to stifle their laughter, to amazement and wonder, and then finally to absolute horror. Some of them even had their hands over their eyes, as if trying to shield themselves from the embarrassing sight in front of them.

Finally, Mr Grimes followed their gaze and turned behind him to see what was so funny. He watched in amazement at the boy who was behaving as if he was possessed.

"Billy, what is wrong with you!" he exclaimed, his anger forgotten in his astonishment.

Billy turned around to face the class. Quick as lightning Peter slipped behind him and caught the back of his tracksuit bottom. With a quick tug, he pulled it down and Billy was left standing with his pants down around his ankles. An unplanned bonus was that Billy was not wearing any underpants that day. The whole lot was on view.

Billy quickly bent down to pull up his pants, desperately trying to cover himself with his hands but he must have realised that the itch was coming from something on his pants because after a second, he let them fall to the ground again and resumed his scratching.

Peter nearly laughed out loud. Now for the final part of his revenge. He took the stink bomb out of his pocket and opened it. A vile smell spread quickly from Billy to Mr Grimes and slowly to the front row of the classroom. The children blocked their noses and coughed. It really was a disgusting smell – like rotten eggs; the strongest farty smell ever. Mr Grimes opened his mouth to say something to address this bizarre sequence of events, but before he could say anything Peter spoke again from behind Billy. "Sir, you smell."

Chapter 12

Mr Grimes looked increduously at Billy. He could see him clearly now. There was something about this whole series of events that was making him very uneasy. Billy had not said those words – he could now see that the boy's lips hadn't moved. He looked like he was possessed. Mr Grimes had read about people being possessed and this definitely looked like such a case. His pants were down around his ankles, he was as white as a sheet, and voices were coming from him that were not being spoken by him. A sudden feeling of terror overcame Mr Grimes – he had to get out of there.

So, to the surprise of the entire class, instead of attacking Billy, Mr Grimes cautiously tiptoed around him, giving him a wide berth, and made for the door.

The whisperings of the class followed him.

"Did you hear what Billy said to Mr Grimes? He's so cheeky!"

"Where is Mr Grimes going? He looks terrified!"

"How is Billy making him leave like that!"

Mr Grimes scuttled out, only pausing to carefully lock the door behind him. A big cheer went up in the classroom. But almost immediately the cheer reverted again to laughter as the boy's attention was drawn back to Billy, whose pants were still down around his ankles. He stood there, miserably looking for a way to escape.

Mr Grimes made his way hurriedly down to the principal's office and told him as much of the bizarre story as he could. The words were choking in his mouth as he tried to splutter them out as quickly as possible.

"What are you talking about, Mr Grimes?" said the principal, looking slightly shocked. "The boy is possessed? Have you gone completely mad? You're not yourself Mr Grimes. You're most dishevelled and you're babbling!"

"It's true, it's true!" cried Mr Grimes. "I saw him with my own eyes! And I heard him too. I have him locked in the classroom."

"Really?" said the principal. "Still in the classroom? Well, let's get to the bottom of this and check it out now."

The two men made their way back to the classroom, approaching the door cautiously. They peered in through the glass and watched the boys. The class was in uproar; children were shouting at the top of their voices and paper airplanes were flying in every direction. And there, in the corner was the boy, Billy. Just as Mr Grimes had said, his pants were down around his ankles. He had stopped jumping around and scratching, but the damage that he had caused to himself was visible in his red and almost bleeding butt cheeks. His hands were in front of himself and he was doing his best to cover up. Some of the boys were teasing him and he looked most upset. The principal stepped forward to enter the classroom, but Mr Grimes abruptly caught him by the sleeve. "Stop," he said. "Do you hear that voice?"

The principal paused, his head to one side, listening intently.

"Billy's got no pants on, Billy's got no pants on!" came a sing-song voice from the direction of Billy.

"That voice isn't coming from Billy," said Mr Grimes, earnestly.

"It must be, there's nobody else near him," said the principal, with a frown.

"It isn't Billy. Can you not see that his lips aren't moving? And he's hardly going to be jeering at himself."

"Hmm …" said the principal, staring intently at Billy. "Hang on a sec, I recognise that voice. That's Peter's voice. I'm sure it is. He's in there somewhere. But where is he? There's nobody near Billy."

"That's what I was trying to tell you!" said Mr Grimes, triumphantly.

"There's something strange going on in there," said the principal after a moment. "I think we need to call the police." He removed his hand from the door handle and turned to Mr Grimes.

"Well done Mr Grimes, for locking the door," he said. "Come down to my office and we'll call the cops. You stay with me in case they have any questions."

Mr Grimes, recovering from his earlier shock, began to compose himself. He was feeling rather important now. He ran a hand through his wiry, wild hair in an attempt to smoothen it. "Of course, Principal Stafford. I'm right here behind you," he said.

The two men hurried back to the office and made the call to the local police station.

"Sergeant Coppers please!" said the principal. "It's regarding the missing boy."

Sergeant Coppers voice came on the phone a moment later.

"You found the boy? Where was he? Oh, you haven't found the boy, but you think he is speaking from the body of another boy? You do realize how crazy that sounds?"

"I know it sounds crazy but I've no other explanation," replied the principal. "It's definitely Peter's voice and he's not in the room."

"Ok - we're on our way," said Sergeant Coppers. "Don't go down to the classroom; stay in your office. I don't want anyone in the class to be suspicious."

The principal put the phone down and the two men sat and waited.

Chapter 13

Secret Agent Boyle sat in his big leather chair in the offices of the agency, thoughtfully rubbing his stubbly chin. He had been working as a secret agent for many years and had investigated some really bizarre claims – haunted buildings, UFO sightings and even alien abductions – but he had never before had reports similar to the one that was presently sitting on his desk. The front cover of the report said, 'Top Secret – For Your Eyes Only' and inside was the title, 'Invisible Forces'. The previous evening, he had received a strange phone call from a police man. He said that people were calling into his station, reporting events of the most peculiar nature in his village; bags flying through the air by themselves; people saying that they had held something alive that they could not see; and even haunted ferris wheels. Normally in such circumstances, there turned out to be a perfectly rational explanation, but events that could possibly involve invisible forces had to be checked out by the agency.

Agent Boyle had given the police man his private phone number, so he could get him at any time and asked him to contact him immediately if he had any more news. So, when the phone on his desk rang, Agent Boyle's hand shot out and grabbed it, like it was the last biscuit in an orphange.

"Sargent Coppers? It's me, Agent Boyle. Have you got some news?"

"Good afternoon, Agent Boyle. Well, I think so. I just got a call from the principal of the local school, St Albans. He says that there is … let me see now, how did he describe it … yes, a demon in the classroom."

"What?"

"He says that there's a boy in the class who's behaving very strangely, and voices are coming from him, even though he's not speaking the words."

"Voices?"

"Yes, that's what he said. Strange voices. He sounded quite alarmed on the phone and he said he locked the door of the classroom before he left. So, whatever was in the classroom is still there."

"Well, I was expecting something more substantial than a boy saying strange things, but since both teachers were spooked and he's still in the classroom, we'll check it out. We'll be there shortly."

Agent Boyle made a quick phone call to two of his colleagues, Agent Black and Agent Matthews, and grabbing their black trench coats and dark glasses, they headed off to the school.

"If there's something in that classroom," said Agent Boyle. "We're going to get it. We have to get to the bottom of this."

Half an hour later they pulled up in front of the school and parked next to a police car that had arrived ahead of them. A cop was leaning against his car, talking to two excited men, and writing in a black notebook. When the car approached, he snapped the notebook shut and walked over to them.

"Good afternoon. I'm Sargeant Coppers," said the police man, shaking their hands. "And this is the prinicipal of the school, Principal Stafford. And Mr Grimes … the teacher who reported the incident." They all shook hands solomnly.

"This better be interesting, dragging us all the way out here," said Agent Boyle gruffly.

"Well, all I can say is that something is going on in that room that's not normal … really spooky in fact," said Mr Grimes. "You'll see for yourself when you get there."

"And just watch out for the boy in the corner," said the principal as he led the way to the boy's classroom. "He's the one who's acting so strangely."

They walked briskly down the corridor but as they approached the classroom, Agent Boyle stopped them.

"That's all right now," he said. "Thank you, gentlemen. We'll take it from here. No, Sargeant, you can wait with the principal in his office."

Sargeant Coppers looked most taken aback and the teachers were very disappointed that they were going to miss all the action, but Agent Boyle was firm. He didn't want anyone knowing about whatever he was going to find in that classroom.

"We'll send the boys out to you one by one," Agent Boyle told them. "Please question them about what they saw."

Mr Grimes, the Principal and Sargeant Coppers walked reluctantly back to the principal's office. As soon as they were out of sight, Agent Boyle turned to the other two agents.

"Agent Black. I want you to stay at this door. Nobody passes through this door unless I say so. Agent Matthews, you come inside with me."

The men unlocked the door and entered the room. Agent Boyle's shrewd eyes swivelled from left to right as he analysed the scene in front of him. He hadn't been in a classroom for over thirty years. The noise! The boys were running around all over the place; crawling under the tables and climbing over them. In the corner was a sorry looking boy with his pants down. *He must be the one with the itch,* he thought. They must be careful not to get too close to him in case it was contagious. It wouldn't do to have three grown men in a similar situation, with their pants down, scratching!

****

When Peter heard the door opening and saw the three men in black entering and then the door being locked again, the smile left his face. *Uh oh, what's going on?* he thought. *Who are those men? What are they doing here and why did they lock the door?* This was not part of his plan. He glanced over at the heavy sash windows wondering if he could escape that way, but judging from the thick cobwebs and dirty flaking paint falling off them, they hadn't been opened for years. He certainly had never seen them opened before. And even if he did manage to open one, the men would be over at the window immediately, if they saw it moving on its own. There was no escape route; he was trapped.

Standing at the top of the classroom, wearing a forbidding black trench coat and dark glasses, the tallest man waited silently. He removed the glasses and his steely blue eyes travelled slowly around the room, resting for a moment on each boy as he scrutinised their behaviour. The boys stopped talking and joking with each other and turned their gaze instead on the ominous stranger. He didn't have to say anything. It was as if invisible rays shot from those piercing eyes, zapping each boy into silence, one by one.

Drawing himself up to his full height, the man finally introduced himself. His voice was loud, and each word was crisp and sharp. "Good afternoon boys. My name is Agent Boyle. I want to ask you all a few questions and then you can meet your teacher at the principal's office."

He had the boy's attention. What was he going to ask them?

"You … boys," he said to Billy and Dean. "You stay just where you are."

He turned to the other man who was standing behind him and whispered to him. The second man nodded solemnly and left the room. Then Agent Boyle called each boy to the front of the classroom. He shook their hand and asked them a different question about what had happened that morning.

"Billy told teacher to stop farting!" said one boy, whispering as he said the word 'farting'."

"Really?" said Agent Boyle.

"Yes. And then he just started scratching his butt for no reason! And he went completely mad, calling teacher names!"

Eager to tell their version of the events, all the boys started talking over each other.

"He told Mr Grimes to stop shouting, but it was *him* who was shouting!"

"Mr Grimes nearly hit him."

"I think a wasp was in his pants. He was trying to get them off as fast as possible. But then I think he got stung."

It was quite surprising, all the differing accounts of just how cheeky Billy had been, but the general drift was of an out of control boy who had frightened the teacher out of the room. None of them could tell exactly what the teacher had been so frightened of.

One by one, the boys were passed to Agent Black at the door and were then told to leave. Finally, there was just one boy left sitting down. Billy and Dean were still standing in the corners. The last boy was Olly.

****

Olly stood up nervously and walked up to the men. He had seen everything and knew who was behind all this. He was Peter's best friend, after all. He recognized Peter's hand writing and had laughed when he saw the writing on the window.

And then he heard the voice; nobody else seemed to recognise it. It was obvious to Olly that it was Peter. So, it was true – he wasn't joking. Somehow, he had made himself invisible. How cool was that? But how had he done it? He couldn't wait to ask him.

And then the pranks had started on Billy. Oh, that was priceless. *Peter must be having a great time,* Olly had thought. He wished he could shout over to him, but Peter obviously didn't want anyone to know it was him, so Olly kept quiet, waiting for class to be over so that they could laugh about it together. They were going to have such fun if Peter had this new superpower. Maybe later, he could show Olly how to do it too.

But right now, Peter would want to stop messing around and become visible again. The way he was carrying on, he was going to be in big trouble.

Chapter 14

From the corner of the room, Peter watched as Olly walked slowly up to the man and stood in front of him. Agent Boyle shook his hand and gripped his shoulder as if to confirm that Olly was a normal boy and that there was nothing weird about him. There was an uncomfortable pause as his shrewd eyes bored through Olly, never looking away and never blinking. Then the eyes narrowed, and he leaned forward, pulling Olly close.

"Come here, boy," he said. "So, you're friends with the missing boy Peter, then."

"Yes sir, but I don't know anything!" Olly stammered. "I haven't seen him since he disappeared."

Just then the door opened and the man who had left earlier, entered the room. In horror, Peter saw that he had a dog on a lead! It was an Alsatian – one of those really scary dogs that looks more like a wolf. The dog was straining on the lead and the man was using all his strength to hold him in check.

Agent Boyle turned to the three boys who were left in the room, Olly, Dean and Billy.

"All right boys, you can all leave," he said.

The three boys turned to leave the room, looking relieved to be away from the scrutiny of the formidable man. Billy waddled out, his pants still down around his ankles and one hand still scratching his bum.

Olly left the room too, but anxiously peeped back through the glass in the door as if worried that Peter might need some help.

Peter certainly could have done with some help. The man who had just entered the room, had one of Peter's t-shirts in his hand. He recognised the blue shark on the front of it. *How did he get that?* Peter wondered. And then the man pressed the t-shirt against the dog's nose. *Oh no!* Peter thought. *He's going to smell me out!*

Peter was right. The man let the dog smell the scent on the t-shirt for a minute and then said, "Go get him, Rover!"

There was no hesitation from the big Alsatian. He made a bound in the direction of Peter. He was enormous; he looked like he could tear him apart in two minutes. His savage teeth were bared, and he made choking sounds as he strained against his chain. Drool dripped from his jaws as if he couldn't wait to get his teeth into Peter's juicy flesh.

"Stop! I'm over here," Peter cried out in terror.

"Did you hear that?" said Agent Boyle to Agent Black, and in a louder voice he said to Peter. "Where … where are you and what are you?"

"I'm here. I'm Peter. Take that dog away and I'll come over to you."

The man quickly signalled to Agent Black to take the dog away.

"Down, Rover," Agent Black said, and immediately the dog lay down at his feet. His tongue hung out placidly as he panted and wagged his tail. It was difficult to believe that this dog had been such a savage beast just a few moments ago.

"Come on, come on! Over here! Hurry up!" said Agent Boyle, impatiently.

"I'm coming," replied Peter nervously, and he dragged his feet across the room to the men. They were waving their hands in front of them like blind men, trying to feel the owner of the mystery voice. Peter was starting to panic. Secret agents with dogs – he was really in trouble now.

"Got him," said Agent Boyle, as his strong hands grabbed Peter's arm. "Wow! What's going on here? How did you do this to yourself?"

Towering down at him from his great height, Secret Agent Boyle's cold eyes bored through him.

"Agent Matthews!" he called. "I have him. He feels just like a normal boy. He's wearing a jumper!"

Agent Matthews approached quickly, patting Peter through his jumper.

"What the heck?" he said in amazement. "I've never seen anything like this before. How did he do this?"

"It's just not possible," muttered Agent Boyle, clumsily patting Peter's invisible face. "We've got to find out how he did this before anyone else finds out. As far as I'm aware, nobody else knows about him yet. Then, we'll get the credit!"

"Hellooo? I can hear, you know," said Peter.

"What do you mean, the credit?" said Agent Matthews. "Do you mean we could get rich? Should we tell the boss?"

"I don't know what exactly we'll get out of this," said Agent Boyle. "Maybe a promotion or maybe large sums of money. But what I do know is that nobody's to know about it. This is huge. If we can manage to find out how he did this before the TV gets wind of it, we'll be millionaires!" He paused and rubbed his chin thoughtfully.

"Ok boy, we're going to take you with us now," he continued, finally addressing Peter. "Just quietly come with us. We don't want anyone to know about you. We've a lot of work to do on you."

"Work to do *on* me? What do you mean work *on* me?" demanded Peter.

"Oh, I meant work *for* you," said Secret Agent Boyle quickly. Peter looked at him uncertainly. Agent Boyle took a pair of handcuffs out of his pocket. He put one on Peter's wrist, and the other on his own wrist so that they were handcuffed together. There was no way that Peter could break free.

"Now if you do anything," he said. "Rover will know before you even think about doing it, and I don't want to have to clean up any messes!"

Clean up any messes! thought Peter. *What was he on about?* There was no way he was going to try any tricks. He didn't want to be turned into a 'mess'. He would just do as they asked and follow them quietly.

"And don't say a word when we talk to your teacher," said Agent Boyle, sternly. "You're coming with us."

The three men, Peter and the dog marched down the corridor to the principal's office where Mr Grimes and the principal were waiting. The teachers looked up with expectancy.

"Principal Stafford," said Agent Boyle in his most authoritative voice. "Agent Black will inform you of the details of our inspection of the classroom. I'll head on to the car with the dog."

He moved off briskly. Peter thought about crying out to the principal for help, but the dog growled and bared his teeth at him as if to say, "Don't even think about it." The handcuff tugged at Peter's arm and he was forced to move off with Agent Boyle and the dog. As he passed by the teachers, Agent Boyle pulled his sleeve down, trying to conceal the handcuff that was attached to his wrist. It was sticking out sideways in a most peculiar fashion, as it connected to Peter's invisible wrist.

Agent Black stopped to explain to the principal that there was nothing out of the ordinary with the class. "Just standard classroom antics with some itching powder and wild imaginations. You can go back and carry on as normal."

Mr Grimes looked confused but turned and headed back to the class. Peter left the building with Agent Boyle and the dog, with a terrible fear in his heart.

Chapter 15

Agent Boyle tugged at the handcuff, urging Peter to move faster as he led him to the car outside. He put the dog in the boot and then sat Peter beside him in the back seat of the car. They waited in silence for the return of Agent Black and Agent Matthews.

"Where are we going?" asked Peter, after a moment.

Agent Boyle jumped and stared at the blank space beside him. He reached out and felt around for Peter's arm as if to reassure himself that this was not all a dream.

"Em ... not far. We've just a few questions to ask you," he said. "You're quite safe."

Peter didn't feel safe. They were complete strangers. He was handcuffed to this weird man and they were going to drive off with him to an unknown place. It had all the elements of a horror movie.

"Where is he?" said Agent Black, as he returned with Agent Matthews and sat in the front seat.

"He's here beside me," said Agent Boyle.

Agent Black turned around and stared through Peter. "Crazy stuff," he said, shaking his head in disbelief.

There was no talk in the car during the journey, but Agent Boyle kept up an intense stare at the position where Peter was sitting. Peter became more and more worried. He anxiously tried to think of a plan of escape. Maybe he could jump out when the car stopped at the traffic lights? They would never find him once he was out of the car. But a movement from

Agent Boyle's arm reminded Peter of the handcuffs and he realised that there was no way he could escape while they were on him.

Agent Boyle must have the key to the handcuffs, he thought, looking at his heavy black coat. *It's probably in one of his pockets. Maybe I could pick pocket him.* He'd never tried this before, but he'd seen people do it in the films and it didn't look very difficult.

As they appoached the next bend in the road, Peter had his hand ready, just touching the edge of Agent Boyle's pocket. Agent Boyle was staring straight ahead at the road, deep in thought. As they rounded the corner, Peter fell against him heavily, slipping his hand into the pocket at the same time.

"Oh, sorry," said Peter, sitting back upright. "That was a sharp bend."

"That's ok," said Agent Boyle. "We're nearly there."

The pocket was empty. There was no key.

Drat it, thought Peter. *It must be in the other pocket.* He was stuck for the moment, but he would be ready if he saw another opportunity to escape.

They drove on through two villages and along a country road and finally, they pulled up in front of a run down, gloomy house. Tall hedges surrounded the house ensuring complete privacy, although Peter couldn't see why privacy was necessary as there were no other houses in sight.

They entered the house and brought Peter to a small room at the back; a dark room, with no windows. The temperature dropped as they entered the room and Peter wrinkled his nose at the damp smell that hung in the air. Hanging from the middle of the ceiling, a bare bulb cast a dim glow around the room. He looked around with distaste. On the left side, there was a small table with two chairs - one on either side of the table. And in the corner, there was a bed. It was a sort of hospital type bed; with an iron headboard and a thin mattress.

"This is where you'll stay, Peter," said Agent Boyle curtly. "Here, put this jumper on." He undid the hand cuff from his own wrist and put a blue jumper over Peter's head. "That's better," he said. "Now we can see where you are."

Peter looked down at the jumper which was now a second jumper because he was already wearing one. It was strange to see his body again.

"Actually, take off the jumper that you have on underneath, so we can send it for analysis," said Agent Boyle.

"All right then," said Peter. "But I want it back!"

"I'll have it back for you in a few days."

"A few days?" said Peter. "How long will I be staying here?"

"Oh, not long. We just want to find out how this happened, Peter. Now, put out your other arm so I can fasten these." He grabbed the handcuff that was dangling from Peter's wrist and snapped Peter's two hands together.

"Hey," said Peter bravely. "Is that really necessary? It's not like I can jump out the non-existent window. And I don't have ghostly powers of walking through walls! They hurt!"

"It's for your own good!" Agent Boyle replied, impatiently.

Handcuffs for my own good? Really? thought Peter with a scowl. But then Agent Boyle's face changed, and he stopped frowning. He bent down to Peter's level, putting his hand on Peter's shoulder. "I've never in my long career seen anything like this before. Peter, think of the money that we can make together if we can reproduce this phenomenon. We'll be billionaires! We'll be famous and on every TV screen! You just have to trust me." A small smile flitted across his face and he looked distantly at the ceiling as though he was imagining the flash of the TV cameras.

Peter didn't know what to think. One minute Agent Boyle was terrifying, shouting at him, and the next he was acting like he was Peter's friend. Could he trust this man? But he called himself Agent Boyle - a secret agent. And certainly, in all the films Peter had seen, secret agents were always the good guys. He must be safe with him.

"Now, Agent Black will bring you some food and a drink" said Agent Boyle. "I presume you do still eat?"

"Yes," said Peter. "Of course, I eat. I'm alive, you know."

"Ok. Well, eat up and go to sleep on that bed over there. We've got a busy day tomorrow."

"How am I going to sleep or eat with these on?" said Peter.

Agent Boyle frowned in irritation. "You'll manage."

Ten minutes later Agent Black arrived in the door. In his hand there was a brown paper bag, and as he entered the room, a pungent odour followed him. It reminded Peter of the smell that came from his feet after they had spent a few hours in wet welly boots.

"Here's your grub," Agent Black muttered, shoving the package towards Peter.

Peter hungrily looked inside the brown bag, hoping the smell wasn't coming from it, but he recoiled as the stench hit him in the face. Inside the bag were some crackers with cheese on the top. He had seen cheese like that once before when his mother had bought a new type to try it out. It was cream in colour and had blueish lumps through it. His mother explained they were actually lumps of blue mould. The cheese had stayed in the fridge for a week and every evening his mother took a slice and spread it on a cracker. The whole fridge stank of rot every time the door was opened. Peter had secretly called it "Bum breath cheese" because anyone who ate it also reeked.

"I can't eat that," Peter said, gagging on the smell.

"Fine," said Agent Black, putting the bag on the table. "I'll just leave it here in case you change your mind."

He stood up and left the room, leaving Peter all alone.

Chapter 16

Sargeant Coppers sat behind his desk, staring at the ceiling, deep in thought. A full cup of coffee lay in front of him, cold and untouched. The pressure was mounting. It had been three days since the boy had gone missing and even though he had put all his efforts into finding him, there was no sign of the boy anywhere. It was as if he had just vanished into thin air. But boys didn't vanish into thin air.

A rap on the door disturbed him from his thoughts and his boss entered, closing the door behind him.

"Any leads on the missing boy, Sargeant Coppers?" he asked.

"No, boss." Sargeant Coppers picked up his notes. "There've been no sightings of him from the advertisements in the newspaper and none from the TV either."

"You must be missing something. If he isn't found soon, then he probably hasn't run away. It's more likely that he's been kidnapped or worse still, killed. Time's running out for finding him safe."

"There *is* something that's niggling me."

"What's that?"

"Well, it might be nothing, but I just have this feeling that something happened inside the classroom. That man, Agent Boyle, left the room very quickly and he didn't speak to anyone when he drove away."

"Well, he might have just been busy and thought we were wasting his time."

"But now I can't reach him," said Sargeant Coppers. "I called his phone loads of times but it's going straight to voice mail. I telephoned his office, but he hasn't turned up at work. It's like he's just disappeared too."

"That's odd, all right, considering that he gave you his emergency phone number to call him on."

"And then there are the teachers," continued Sargeant Coppers, hardly aware of his boss as he puzzled over the events. "Mr Grimes was absolutely sure that he heard the boy, Peter, in his classroom and the principal backed him up. And you know very well that when two people tell the same story, it isn't necessarily true, but it's less likely to be imagined by them."

"You should have checked out that room before calling the secret agent," said his boss, with a frown.

"I know. I'm really annoyed with myself. If I'd done so, I wouldn't be sitting here now, scratching my head. I would have seen for myself what was going on. I won't be making that mistake again."

"Well did you get *anything*?"

Sargeant Coppers took his phone out of his pocket and looked through the photos. "I haven't much to go on. The only bit of useful information that I got is a photo of the number plate on Agent Boyle's car."

"Forget Agent Boyle. There's no point looking for a grown man when you could be losing valuable time finding the boy. Locating Peter is your top priority."

Sargeant Coppers closed his phone and put it back in his pocket. "You're right… Well then, I'll go and pay a visit to Peter's parent's house. They don't seem to be concerned at all about their missing son."

"Yes, do that. When a child goes missing, a close relative is usually the culprit. And they're an odd pair."

"All right, boss. Leave it with me." Sargeant Coppers pushed aside the papers on his desk and looked for his little black book; the one he kept everyone's address in.

****

Not far away, in a dark room, Peter was feeling bad. Being chained up like a dog was not fun. He lay awake for most of the night, tossing and turning in the uncomfortable bed as he thought of how he was going to get out of this situation. Even if Agent Boyle was to be trusted, he was making life very uncomfortable for him. A painful rash had developed on the back of his neck from the itchy blue woollen jumper, and the stink in the room from the cheese added to his bad mood.

At half past six in the morning he was greeted by Agent Boyle, who seemed so excited by the thoughts of the day, he looked like could hardly contain himself. His eyes were wide and bright, and he almost ran over to Peter's bed to make sure he was still there, and it hadn't all been a dream.

"Wake up, Peter," he said, roughly shaking him by the arm. "I have breakfast for you and then we'll get straight down to work."

Peter sat up and scowled at him. "This jumper is itching me like crazy. I'm not wearing it anymore."

"Ok. You can take it off. And I'll take those off you too," said Agent Boyle, pointing to the handcuffs. He unlocked the handcuffs and Peter got up and inspected his breakfast. *Toast - good. And tea.*

"Hey... what's that?" said Agent Boyle, pointing in alarm as Peter started to eat.

"What's what?" asked Peter, with his mouth full. "My chewed-up toast? Yeah, that freaked me out a bit too, the first time I saw it."

"Wow," said Agent Boyle in awe, watching what looked like a small ball of chewed up bread turning around and around in the air all by itself. He put a pair of sunglasses on the table.

"Here, put these on so I know where your head is."

Peter obligingly put the sunglasses on and continued eating. It wasn't very comfortable trying to eat with a strange man staring at every mouthful as he chewed and swallowed. Agent Boyle was writing furiously as he muttered.

"The food is the only thing visible where the patient's head should be. It can be seen to be chewed and swallowed in ball shapes as they pass down to the stomach. The food forms a sludgy mass in the stomach as it presumably mixes with the stomach acid. The stomach acid itself is not visible."

Peter swallowed the last gulp of tea. Suddenly he didn't feel like eating. All this talk of "sludge" and "stomach acid" was putting him off his food.

"Now, Peter. I have some questions," said Agent Boyle, pulling his chair up close and looking intently at the pair of sunglasses floating in mid air. "Who knows about you?"

"What do you mean? Loads of people know me. My parents, everyone at school, uncles, aunts…"

"I mean about you being invisible, of course! Did you tell anyone?"

"No, I don't think anyone knows. It only happened yesterday."

Agent Boyle's eyes became brighter and he leaned closer, firing out questions so fast that Peter had barely time to answer.

"Did it ever happen before, or was this the first time?"

"This is the first time."

"How did you do it?"

"I just wished for it."

"Ok… that's obviously not true, but we'll come back to that. Can you become visible again?"

"I don't think so."

"Where are your parents?"

"At home, I presume."

"Are they expecting you back?"

"I'm a boarder at the school."

"So, they're not expecting you back. Hmmm… very good. Why did you run away from school?"

"I was in trouble with the teacher."

"Did the man in the market cast a spell on you?"

"He might have. It's always a possibility."

"Well, did you see him use anything? Any spell paraphernalia, like…" Agent Boyle paused trying to think. "No wands, no newt's eyes? Or maybe magic words being spoken?"

"Are you actually serious? That's only in fairy tales."

The questions went on and on for about an hour. Peter answered as best he could but couldn't help him with the answer as to how he had actually become invisible. This was obviously the most critical piece of information, as Agent Boyle was never going to become a billionaire without it. As his patience started to wear thin, he grabbed Peter by the shoulders and shook him hard, lowering his angry face close to Peters and baring his teeth. "You do know! Stop lying. I'll set the dog on you and he'll tear you apart. Tell me or I'll punch you!"

"I don't know!" said Peter, shocked at the sudden outburst. "Please sir, I'm telling the truth!" He glanced around, desperately wondering how he was going to get out of this situation. Agent Boyle was behaving most alarmingly.

Agent Boyle's cold blue eyes stared unblinking into Peter's tear-stained eyes. He held the gaze for what seemed like an eternity, his face inches from Peters, his eyes boring like two drills into him. But finally, Agent Boyle gave up and tried a different tactic.

"Ok Peter, sit up on the bed. We're going to do some tests."

Peter was relieved. He was getting quite scary. He sat on the bed and Agent Boyle brought out a note book. 'Samples' was written on the top of the page. He then produced a test tube, and asked Peter to spit into it while he carefuly wrote "Saliva" on the label.

"I need a poo and a wee sample now, Peter," he said handing him two bottles and pointing across the hall to another door. "The toilet's over there."

Peter went over, quickly looking around the small room to see if there was anything that could help him get out of there. A dirty toilet with no toilet paper greeted him, and in the corner, water dripped from a tap into a stained sink. But high up on the wall, there was a small window. Peter looked up at it, trying to calculate if he could squeeze through it. But a cough from Agent Boyle in the next room reminded him that he was being watched like a hawk. He couldn't try it now. He would have to come back later if he got a chance to be on his own. In the meantime, he had some samples to hand over.

The wee sample wasn't so hard to produce and trap in the small bottle, but the poo sample was much harder to deliver. First, he had to squeeze one out, which isn't easy to do on demand. Then he had to try to catch the poo before it fell into the toilet and aim it into this tiny bottle, while all the time trying to keep his hands clean.

Oh, this is disgusting! Peter thought. It was getting all over his hands. It was the only visible thing on his hands, and it stank. Well, he would have some satisfaction giving this bomb to Agent Boyle. Ha! He deserved it for shouting at him so much.

But Agent Boyle was not disgusted as Peter handed over the smelly poo sample. In fact, he looked really pleased.

"Back up on the bed!" Agent Boyle called over.

Peter sat up on the bed again.

"Now, I need a blood sample. Roll up your sleeve." He produced a large needle and held Peter in a tight grip as he felt around his arm. The sight of the needle made Peter felt faint. He wriggled, trying to pull his arm away. That needle was huge!

"Will you stay still!" shouted Agent Boyle. "Ok, that's it. I'll have to strap you down!"

To Peter's horror, Agent Boyle looked under the bed and produced four leather straps.

"No!" Peter shouted at the top of his voice. "Let me go! Help!"

"Shut up," said Agent Boyle, and he quickly strapped Peter's arms and feet to the bed with the four straps. Peter was totally helpless; he couldn't move, stretched out on the bed, like a fly in a spider's web waiting for the spider to approach. Agent Boyle could do whatever he wanted to him and there was no one to hear him.

"Now just behave and I'll have this done in a minute," said Agent Boyle, waving the huge needle in front of him and looking at Peter with a wild glint in his eye.

He felt around and grabbed Peter's arm. Rolling up Peter's sleeve, he started patting what looked like thin air. Peter could see that this wasn't going to be easy. There was no arm to be seen, let alone any veins in which to stick the needle.

"I'm going to have to go for an artery rather than a vein," Agent Boyle muttered, half to himself. "Keep still, Peter, till I find a pulse."

Then Peter felt a sharp prick as Agent Boyle poked around with the needle, trying to guess how deep to insert it. Peter screamed in pain. "Stop, stop! You're hurting me! Aaarrgghh!"

He received a swift slap across the face.

"The noise coming from you! Would you ever be quiet!" said Agent Boyle, and he went back poking at Peter's arm.

After an interminable amount of time, he seemed to be satisfied that he had enough of the sample in his test tube. Peter was sobbing on the bed. What was going to become of him? He had to get out of there!

Agent Boyle labelled the sample and brought out the hand cuffs again. "Ok Peter," he said. "I have to bring these samples to the lab while they're still fresh. We can take those straps off you."

He untied Peter's hands and legs and sat him up in the bed. Peter rubbed his wrists. He could feel two welts on his skin from where he struggled against them.

Suddenly, from behind Agent Boyle, he caught sight of a key sitting on the table. Was that the key of the hand cuffs? Had Agent Boyle left it on the table? Maybe he could get it. He waited until Agent Boyle turned his back and then, quick as lightening, he jumped off the bed and over to the table. He grabbed the key and ran back to the bed, slipping the key under the covers.

Hearing the noise, Agent Boyle looked around, frantically feeling on top of the bed. "What are you doing?" he cried. "Where are you? Get back here!"

"Sorry... I just fell off the bed," Peter said, quickly climbing back up.

"Quick, hands out and put these on before you get up to any of your tricks!" said Agent Boyle.

Peter obediently put out his two arms and Agent Boyle snapped the hand cuffs shut, looping them through the bed post.

"I'll be back later," he said. "And I'll bring you some chocolate. How about that! And you might remember how you did this invisible trick." He drew his thin lips back over his teeth in a poor attempt at a smile. But his eyes remained cold, fixed and expressionless.

"Ok," said Peter. "I'll try to remember." He almost preferred the angry face. This false smiling Agent Boyle was most unnerving.

Agent Boyle stood up and turned away from him.

Go on, go! Peter thought, as Agent Boyle collected his samples and left the house, locking the door behind him. Now was his chance. He might not get an opportunity like this again. He had to quickly get the key and unlock the hand cuffs.

He slid his foot down under the bed clothes and felt around with his toes for the key. Where was it? He had to find it quickly. Agent Boyle wouldn't be gone for long. Frantically, he thrashed his legs around the bed, trying to locate the small key. His useless hands strained against the handcuffs, desperately trying to help.

Finally, he felt cold steel against his ankle. He had it! Stretching his feet and opening his toes, he tried to pick up the key between his big toe and the next toe but every time he thought he had a good grip, it slipped and fell back onto the bed.

Just then he heard a car approaching the house. He froze, wondering who it could be. *Agent Boyle must be back already!* he thought. *He must have forgotten something. I'm not going to get out of here in time!*

He quickly gave up with his toes and tried sliding the key up towards his hands instead. Inch by inch, the key moved slowly up the bed, looking like it was moving all by itself. He panted with the effort as he stretched his legs up as far as he could and pushed his hands down to try to reach them. The handcuffs were tearing into the skin on his arms. But at last the tips of his fingers grasped the tiny key.

A car door slammed outside, and he heard the sound of heavy footsteps approaching the house. With shaking hands, he inserted the key into the keyhole and the handcuff sprang open. He was free!

Jumping off the bed, he ran quickly into the bathroom and climbed up onto the window sill. Through a crack in the window, he could see Agent Boyle outside at the front door, fumbling with a bunch of keys in his hands as he tried to find the correct key for the door. Peter heaved himself up to the window and tried to squeeze through. The window was smaller than he had calculated, or his head was bigger; this was going to be a tight squeeze. He forced his head through, nearly ripping his two ears off. He was going to get stuck!

"Peter! Where are you?" came Agent Boyle's voice from inside the room. He had obviously seen the unlocked hand cuffs and was now desperately searching the room for his prized possession.

He ran into the bathroom just as Peter finally squeezed through the window. He looked up sharply at the rustling sound, watching in horror at the sight of the window moving by itself. "My prize! It's escaping!" he exclaimed, making a grab in the direction of the window and trying desperately to close it before Peter got out.

But he was too late. Peter jumped down outside and ran off as fast as he could go.

Chapter 17

From behind a bush, Peter watched Agent Boyle frantically searching the area. The look of despair on his face was almost pitiful. He had lost this most fascinating scientific miracle and was never going to be a billionaire. He ran off down the road looking for any clues as to where Peter had gone.

There was one more thing that Peter had to do before he headed off. He wanted to make Agent Boyle pay for the pain that he had caused him. God knows what further painful experiments he would have inflicted on him, if he hadn't escaped.

As usual, Peter's creative, mischief-making mind had a cunning plan. The front garden was full of dog poo that hadn't been cleared away. Agent Boyle's car was parked in front of the house. Peter looked around for something to scoop up the poo. He found a flattish stick and scraped some onto the stick. Then, looking all around him to check that there still was no one in sight, he smeared the poo under the car door handle. He then got a leaf to clean the top of the handle, so no one could see what was under it.

Job done! Ha! How he wished he could stay to see the look on Agent Boyle's face when he went to open the car door.

****

Peter was free again. Free, but alone in an unknown place, with no idea how to get back and no way of asking for directions. He stepped out onto the country road and headed off, wondering how long it would take him to get back to the school. The journey in the car had not taken very long so he hoped it wasn't too far.

A car hurtled past, barely missing him and Peter dived into the ditch. He had forgotten that the cars couldn't see him and wouldn't swerve to avoid him. From then on, he cautiously trudged through the long grass in the verge, instead of walking on the road and finally, the ditch disappeared, and a footpath took over as a village came into sight.

In the distance, he could see the outline of a lady making her way slowly towards him, laden down with two shopping bags. He quickened his step with relief. There was no one else around and he really needed confirmation that he was going the right way.

"Excuse me," he called out as soon as she was within earshot. "Is this the right way to St Albans school?"

The minute the words had left his mouth he was aware of how ridiculous the situation was. How could he have forgotten that he was invisible... again?

The poor lady jumped as though a car horn had unexpectedly gone off in her ear. She stared wildly around the empty country road, dropped her bags, and ran back screaming in the direction of the village.

Peter looked at her retreating form, amazed at the effect he was having and wondered what to do with the two shopping bags at his feet.

He picked them up and followed her. "I'm sorry... you forgot your bags!" he called.

The lady looked back over her shoulder and ran even faster. Peter looked down at the two shopping bags bobbing along on their own and realized why she was running away. They looked very odd.

"Leave me alone, please!" she sobbed.

Peter stopped and put down her bags. This wasn't working. Maybe there was a signpost in the village that would show him the way. The lady could get her bags later when she'd recovered.

Leaving the bags on the side of the footpath, he continued to the centre of the village, watching the lady as she disappeared around a corner in the distance.

Up ahead he could see a roundabout and his heart sang with joy when he saw a signpost with "Woodlands, 3km" written on it. Hallelujah! All was not lost. He would be able to find his way back. With a new spring in his step he walked the final distance and arrived at the school gates an hour later. This time he was going to make contact with Olly. He needed his help; he couldn't do this whole invisible survival thing on his own.

****

In the meantime, Olly had been very worried about his friend. He didn't know what to do. That weird man with the ferocious looking dog had gone off in a car with Peter. He couldn't see Peter, but Olly just knew that he'd been caught. What should he do? He could tell his mother, but what if Peter didn't want him to? He was very worried. What was going to happen to his friend? That evening he went home and desperately wracked his brains as to what he should do. His mother noticed that he was very quiet and sat him down.

"Olly, what's the matter?" she said. "Is everything all right at school?" Olly didn't reply. He really wanted to tell her everything, but he didn't know if he should just yet.

"Don't worry," she continued, giving him a hug. "They'll find Peter. He's probably just hiding somewhere, or he's gone to an aunt's or uncle's house."

She held him tightly and he hugged her back.

The following day there was still no sign of Peter at school. Olly entered the classroom feeling hopeful, but his face fell when he saw the empty seat where Peter should have been sitting.

Oh no! What should I do? he thought. *This is going on too long... Maybe Peter's in danger and really needs my help!* He made up his mind that he would tell his mother that evening. He couldn't bear keeping this secret all to himself any longer.

****

When Peter finally arrived at the school, he found his classroom empty; books and chairs were strewn all over the place. He stood there in the peace and quiet wondering where everyone was, but then he remembered that they had PE that afternoon and that they were probably outside playing football. So he sat down on a chair and tried to think of a plan.

After seeing the reaction of the lady in the village, Peter realised that it was going to be difficult to make contact with Olly - and only Olly - without attracting the attention of everyone else. He had to warn Olly about his appearance (or lack of appearance) before he met him so that Olly wouldn't make a scene. But how was he going to do that? He couldn't talk or touch him. He wracked his brains, thinking how it could be achieved and then finally came up with a solution.

"I know!" he thought out loud. "I'll use the secret code. And then only Olly will be able to understand it!"

He went over to the blackboard and wrote in big letters:

"m'i nvisiblei - eetm ouy utsideo het chools ateg"

He put back the chalk and checked the message from the back of the classroom. Yes, it was clearly visible, and Olly would definitely understand what was going on. He left the classroom, went back outside and sat down on the grass to wait for school to finish.

****

Outside in the football pitch, Olly was standing in the goal, watching the ball as it hurtled towards him, as if in slow motion. It walloped him in the chest and bounced back to Ronan.

"Great save, Olly!" someone cried. But Olly only barely heard. His mind was miles away and it was only luck that the ball had hit him in the chest and had not passed into the goal. This was the longest day ever. He really needed to get home to tell his mother about Peter. Time was running out.

At last the game ended and all the boys trooped back into the classroom and sat down. Then Mr Grimes entered, slamming the door behind him. He turned and looked at the blackboard frowning as he puzzled over the badly written scrawl on the board that made no sense.

Olly looked up and immediately saw the strange writing. He recognised that writing - it was a message from Peter in the secret code! He quickly wrote the message down into his copy before Mr Grimes wiped the blackboard clean. In two seconds, Olly had deciphered the code. "I'm invisible – meet you outside the school gate."

His heart jumped with joy. Peter was safe; he was here! He would get to talk to him just as soon as this boring lesson was over.

When the bell finally rang for the end of school, Olly grabbed his bag and was the first one out the classroom door. He walked quickly down the corridor, overtaking the slower boys in front of him. When he got outside, he ran all the way to the front gate and looked around. Groups of parents were standing outside the gate, chatting to each other as they waited for their boys to appear.

Olly scanned the area for anything out of the ordinary that might indicate that Peter was there, but there was nothing out of place. Nobody was behaving suspiciously. He checked around the cars in the car park; no sign of Peter. He frantically ran to the side of the building to see if Peter was around the corner. He even checked behind the bins, but Peter wasn't there. Olly sighed in disappointment. Maybe he had mistaken the code? Maybe Peter hadn't written it?

But just as he turned away, ready to go home, a voice in front of him whispered. "Olly! It's me, Peter! Don't say anything. Just follow me to the tree over there."

Olly jumped in surprise. There was absolutely nothing in front of him where the voice was coming from - just the path and the grass beyond and a big oak tree a little further away. As he looked down at the grass in front of him, he could see patches of it flatten and then spring back up again. That must be Peter's footprints! He followed the footprints to the tree and suddenly something grabbed his hand.

"Olly, I'm here," came the voice of Peter from the air just in front of him. "I know this is really weird, but as you can see, I'm in a bit of trouble."

"You don't say!" replied Olly, peering to see if he could see any sign that somebody was there. "How the heck did you do that? To think that I didn't believe you. You had me really worried! Just become visible again and it will all be ok."

He put his hand out, poking the body that he could not see.

"But that's the problem," said Peter. "I don't seem to be able to reverse it! In fact, I don't even know how it happened in the first place!"

"Ok," said Olly. "Start from the beginning. What exactly have you been up to?"

Chapter 18

Peter hurriedly told him the whole story. Leaving the school, heading to town, trying to steal the doughnut, three men chasing him and then him wishing that he could become invisible. Then he told Olly about hiding under the table and not being able to see any parts of his body!

"It was so weird, Olly," he said. "I really didn't do anything else and suddenly here I am, completely invisible and no one can see me!" Then he told him about retrieving his bag and being chased again and then spending the night in a complete stranger's house.

"That wasn't such a good suggestion of yours, you know … I nearly got caught. I won't be doing that again. Oh, I nearly forgot. I went on a Ferris wheel for free! You really missed out on that one. But, to be honest, the only reason I ended up on the wheel was because Mr Grimes appeared in the town and looked like he was coming after me, so I jumped on the wheel to get away from him."

"That's weird," said Olly. "What was he doing there?"

"I dunno… and of course you know what happened the next day," Peter went on. "That was me, in the class. Good pranks, eh? I really got Billy back for everything that he did to us."

"Yeah," said Olly. "I knew that it was you, all right. I couldn't stop laughing! Billy's never going to be a hard man any more. All we have to say is 'itchy pants' and he'll die of embarrassment!"

They grinned as they remembered the demented look on Billy's face.

"But Peter," continued Olly. "What was the story with those men? I was really worried. They looked really mean, and then I saw the dog!"

"Yeah," said Peter. "That wasn't funny at all."

He told Olly about the dog smelling him out and nearly savaging him, and the car ride with the strange men, and finally about his ordeal, trapped in the house.

"He was going to do experiments on me," said Peter. "He had me tied to the bed and was sticking needles in me trying to get blood samples. I was screaming with the pain, he was at it for so long. He couldn't see my arm where he was poking me with the needle."

"Oh my God, Peter," Olly replied. "That's mad! You can't do that to a child! It's like kidnapping and torture!"

"Well, I'm not sure the laws apply if you can't actually see the person that you're kidnapping or torturing. There's no evidence ... Anyway, the rest is a bit boring. I just walked all the way back and wrote the message on the blackboard. Cool, eh? I knew that our code would come in handy someday."

"But Peter," said Olly, scratching his head. "What are you going to do now?"

"Well, I really need your help, Olly. I've nowhere else to go. My parents don't want me. They'll hand me over to a doctor. The doctor will tell the police, and they'll send me back to Agent Boyle for more experiments. I won't go back there. I can't go back there. I could be left there until he kills! You've got to help!"

"Ok, calm down, Peter. Don't worry. We'll work something out. Just let me think for a second. I just can't get over that fact that I can't see you at all. There's nothing there!"

He put his arms out to feel what looked like empty space.

"I'm here," said Peter, putting Olly's hand on his arm.

"It's just the weirdest thing," said Olly, as he felt him all over. Olly looked like he was practicing sign language, standing all alone, making shapes with his fingers. "Can you feel this?" he said, as he pinched Peter on the arm.

"Ow, yes I can!" replied Peter. "Can you feel this?" He punched Olly on one arm. "Or this?" A punch to the other side.

"Ok, ok, you win," laughed Olly.

They were silent for a minute as they thought about the invisibility problem.

"Peter," said Olly, after a few moments. "We have to tell my mother… we can't do this on our own.

"No!" exclaimed Peter. "You can't do that! No adult can know! Can't you see? They'll just tell the police!"

"But I have to, Peter. How do you think we can manage without telling an adult?"

"I'm invisible!" Peter said. "No one can see me. It'll be fine. I'll stay in your room."

"You can't stay in my house forever and expect that no one will know that you're there. My mum will be fine if we tell her."

"No way," said Peter. "Then I won't go with you."

"All right then," Olly sighed. "I won't say anything for now. Just get in the car when she arrives, and we'll talk about this later."

"Do you promise?"

"I promise," said Olly. "Really, I won't say a word without you saying that it's ok. You can trust me."

Just then, Olly's mother, Mrs Browne, appeared at the school gates.

"Olly!" she called. "I'm over here! Come on!"

"Come on then, Peter," Olly said. "You get into the car first and I'll follow."

The boys followed Olly's mother over to the car.

"Get in the back there and put your seatbelt on," said his mum.

Olly opened the door and Peter slipped into the car. Olly followed, sitting beside him.

"Good day at school, honey?" enquired Olly's mother as they set off.

"Yeah," replied Olly. "Nothing new."

"No news about Peter?"

"No," said Olly quickly, and then added, trying to change the subject, "What's for dinner?"

"Pasta," replied Mrs Browne. She looked questionly at Olly but said nothing more.

They soon arrived at Olly's house and Olly jumped out of the car quickly and opened the house door. Peter followed like a shadow. Olly went straight down to his room and shut the door after Peter.

"Ok... you stay here and read a book or something," said Olly. "I'll bring you some dinner after I've had mine."

"Don't say a word, remember?" said Peter.

"I won't," said Olly. "Back in a few minutes."

Chapter 19

As Mrs Browne slowly stirred the dinner, she frowned, deep in thought about Olly's friend. He had been missing for more than two days now. She could see that Olly was very worried too but didn't know how to console him. She looked up as she heard his approaching footsteps and smiled.

"Dinner's ready, honey."

"Good," replied Olly, avoiding eye contact.

"Olly, what's wrong?" she said. "You're not yourself at all today."

"Nothing," said Olly, quickly.

"You can tell me, Olly," she continued. "You know I won't tell anyone. Is it those bullies at school again?"

"No, I'm fine," replied Olly.

Mrs Browne said nothing more but decided to keep a close eye on him and ask him again later. She watched him as he finished his dinner and noticed that he was hanging round the kitchen instead of shooting off to the computer room, like he normally did. Then he began looking in the cupboards for food.

"Do you want a biscuit, Olly?" she asked.

"Yeah," replied Olly, grabbing a full packet. He skulked out of the kitchen and down to his bedroom.

What is he up to? she thought.

She followed him down to his room, keeping her distance. His bedroom door was closed so she put her ear to the door. She got the surprise of her life when she heard him talking to someone inside. *Who has he in there?* she thought. *It sounds like a child!*

Then she heard him say. "Peter, that's all I could get."

She had to find out what was going on! She burst open the door and marched inside. There was Olly, all by himself, sitting on the bed. A packet of biscuits hovered in the air in front of him.

"Olly! What's going on?" she exclaimed, staring incredulously at the floating packet of biscuits. "Who are you talking to? And *how* are you doing *that?*"

Olly jumped at the sight of his mother and stammered. "Eh … what? Em, nothing's going on."

"Olly!" his mum replied. "I'm not stupid! There's a packet of biscuits floating in the air in front of you. How are you doing that?"

Olly grabbed the biscuits and tried to hide them. But just then a voice said. "Olly, just tell her."

"Olly!" she said. "What's going on? Is there a ghost in here?" She felt the blood drain from her face and her hands started to shake. She went over to the bed for support.

"No, Mum," Olly replied hurriedly. "Calm down. I'll explain everything. But first you have to promise that you won't tell anyone."

"What? Ok … I promise," she said, not really aware of what she was promising.

"This is a bit hard to believe," continued Olly. "But my friend, Peter, is here."

"What? Where?" she said, looking around wildly. "I can't see anyone."

"He's invisible," said Olly.

"I'm right here, Mrs Browne," Peter said, finally speaking up. "I'm in trouble and I need your help."

"Oh my God… what is going on?" cried Mrs Browne, completely baffled. "Peter! Where are you?"

"I told you, he's invisible. That's why you can't see him," Olly explained.

"But how?" said Mrs Browne, perplexed. "How did you do that to yourself?" She stared in front of her, straining to see if there was a shimmer, or anything at all that would indicate that Peter was there. "At least you're safe. You've been found. We better tell the police."

"You can't tell anyone, Mrs Browne," Peter exclaimed. "You promised!"

"Okay, tell me everything," she said, recovering her composure. "From the very beginning. Come over here so I can feel you."

She stretched out her arm and a moment later felt the soft hand of a child, gripping her hand.

"My God, Peter. Are you actually standing in front of me?" she said in amazement. She reached out her other hand and felt a shoulder in her grasp.

"Yes, Mrs Browne."

"But, do you feel ok? Do you feel any different? You don't feel sick?"

"I feel fine… just the same."

"How are we going to get this off you?" she murmured, running her hand over his chest.

"Mum," said Olly. "I hope you're not planning to treat this situation like some dirt that can be scrubbed off with a bit of elbow grease?"

"Well… you never know till you try," she said. "But, tell me Peter. How did this happen to you?"

Peter told the long story from the beginning again, ending by telling her his fear of being sent back to Agent Boyle. Mrs Browne sat with her mouth open as she listened to his story, touching him every now and again to reassure herself that he was really there and that it was not all a bizarre dream. She frowned as he told her about the cruelty of Agent Boyle.

"Oh, I'll kill him!" she said angrily. "How could he do that to a poor defenceless boy? The big bully!"

"So, you see, Mrs Browne," Peter finished finally. "You can't tell anyone. Please! We trusted you!"

Mrs Browne could hear the panic in the small boy's voice. "It's ok, Peter," she said finally. "I won't say anything for the moment. The main thing is that you're here and you're safe. I'll make sure that no one will harm you. I promise."

"Good old Mums," said Olly. "I told you we could trust her."

"But what about your parents?" said Mrs Browne, thoughtfully. "We have to tell them… They must be worried sick. And we need to let the police know so that they can call off the search."

"He can stay with us, Mum," said Olly. "His parents don't want him, and he'll be like my brother! No one needs to know!"

Mrs Browne smiled. If only it was so easy. But Peter was right. There was a high chance that Agent Boyle would get his hands on him if he found him and she was determined that she was not going to let that happen. "Ok boys," she said, as she left the room. I'll have a think about what we will do. In the meantime, I don't want any tricks going on. I do *not* want to come back and find two invisible boys!"

"Ok Mum, we won't do anything," said Olly, as she left the room and closed the door behind her.

****

"Ok, Peter, show me how to do it!" said Olly, as soon as his mum was out of earshot. "I want to be invisible too!" His eyes were bright with excitement.

"Well," said Peter. "All I said was, "Please make me invisible… I'll do *anything*!" and I tried really hard to imagine myself invisible. It just happened then!"

Squeezing his eyes shut tight and trying really hard to imagine that he too was invisible, Olly said the words, but to his great disappointment, nothing happened. When he opened his eyes, he was exactly the same. "Hang on! I'll try again," he said.

Peter watched as Olly tried time after time with no success.

"It's not going to work, Olly," Peter said finally. "Just forget about it. Let's do something else."

"All right," said Olly reluctantly. "I know, let's plan all the pranks we can do with you!"

"Well actually, I was thinking that we could make some money out of this," said Peter. "We could go to a busy street and bring a teddy, or something, and you could say that you were moving the teddy by mind control!"

"Yeah," said Olly, enthusiastically. "That's a great idea. Just imagine the faces on the people when they see the teddy dancing all by himself. It could even beg for money. And we could have our own magic show. We'd make loads of money!"

"And we could freak out Mr Grimes again," said Peter. "I think he'd be afraid to go back into the classroom if more weird, spooky stuff was to happen again!"

"That was funny, all right," said Olly. "Did you see the colour he went when he discovered that Billy wasn't actually saying those words to him? I thought he was going to faint!"

The two boys chatted away happily all night, planning all the endless possibilities for fun. They didn't give a further thought as to how Mrs Browne was going to deal with the situation of keeping a secret invisible boy in her house.

****

Mrs Browne, on the other hand was awake all night, trying to think what could be done with Peter. She knew that harbouring a missing child in her house was a crime. It was effectively a kidnapping situation. She would go to prison if it was found out. It would also be very difficult to keep this secrecy up for any length of time. People were looking for Peter. He had parents who must be really worried. She didn't know what she would do if it had been Olly that was missing for so long. She'd be sick with worry. But she was also very worried about Peter, and especially that story of the secret agent men who had been so cruel to him. If they found

Peter again, they would definitely do more experiments on him to try to explain this scientific phenomenon.

She had also made a promise to the boys and she really didn't want to go behind their backs and be a traitor. She tossed and turned in bed all night and finally came to the decision that she would have to persuade Peter to let her bring him back to his parent's house. She was sure that if she explained how frightened Peter was, that they would protect him, as every parent should. First of all, though, she would try to make him visible   again...

Chapter 20

Next morning everyone woke up early. Mrs Browne called the school to say that Olly was sick, so he could stay at home with Peter for the day. Then she called the boys and told them to have a bath. Mrs Browne had a huge jacuzzi bath so both boys jumped in together. It was so weird to see the water part around Peter's feet when he stepped into the bath leaving two hollow shapes in the water. When he stood up, drops of water stayed on his invisible body and as he moved, the wispy shape of a boy could be seen in the form of water droplets.

Mrs Browne got to work straight away. She was armed with a strong cleaning solution and a rough sponge.

"Come here, Peter," she said. "Let's see if we can get this off you."

She held him by the arm and started sponging where she thought his back was. It was a bit like polishing a very clean window. Peter felt solid but she could see straight through him. Mrs Browne was good at cleaning things. She had years of experience with dirty cookers and floors and took pride in her spotless house. But her skills were failing her now. No matter how hard she tried, there was no sign of Peter's skin appearing.

"That's getting kind of sore, Mrs Browne," Peter said after a while. "My skin is nearly rubbed raw. I don't think it's working."

"No," sighed Mrs Browne reluctantly. "I suppose you're right. So that option is ruled out." She stretched out her hand and flexed her fingers. "And my arm is aching from all that scrubbing."

Just then there was a knock at the front door - a loud authoritative knock.

Mrs Browne looked around anxiously. Suddenly her heart was beating very fast. Who could be at the door? Oh no! If she was found out, she was going to be in deep trouble with the police! Oh, why had she let Peter stay the night? She should have called the police immediately when he had arrived   yesterday.

The knock on the door sounded again.

"Stay there, boys, and don't say a word to anyone," said Mrs Browne. Her hands were shaking now. She walked down the hall and opened the door. Two police men stood there.

"Good morning, Mrs Browne," said the first police man. "My name is Sargeant Coppers. I'm sure you are aware that a boy is missing, and we are doing house to house searches to try to find him."

"No… I mean, yes. Yes, I heard that there is a missing boy," Mrs Browne stammered, feeling her face flush.

"Oh, you *heard*, did you? He is apparently a very close friend of your son's," continued the policeman, looking suspiciously at her red nervous face.

"Is he? I didn't really know that. Olly has a lot of friends," Mrs Browne mumbled.

"Really? You don't know Peter? How strange," said Sargeant Coppers, consulting his black notebook. "I have information here to say that he was at a birthday party here in February, and last year too, and the year before? You are still quite sure that you don't know him?"

Mrs Browne squirmed. "Oh, *that* Peter," she said. "Eh, yes, I do know him."

Sargeant Coppers looked at her closely. "Mrs Browne," he said. "We are going to check your house. Please stand aside."

"Of course, Sargeant," said Mrs Browne, trying to keep the panic out of her voice. "There's just my boy, Olly here. He's not in school today because he's eh, kind of sick."

Mrs Browne felt sick too, sick from worry and panic. How was she going to get out of this?

Sargeant Coppers and the other policeman stepped past Mrs Browne in the doorway and started to check each room quickly. They soon came to the bathroom.

"I'm in here!" called out Olly, trying to prevent them from entering the room.

"All right, son," called Sargeant Coppers. "Dress yourself and let us in."

"Excuse me," said Mrs Browne, as she pushed past him. "I'll just check he's got his clothes with him."

She went in and closed the door behind her.

"It's the police!" she whispered, looking wildly around. "Don't tell them anything!"

Olly got out of the bath and put his clothes on.

"Peter, get out of the bath and dry yourself," Mrs Browne said. "You're not completely invisible with the water drops on you!"

Peter jumped out of the bath, grabbed a towel and dried himself quickly.

"Two seconds!" called out Olly. "Just putting my pants on!"

Peter moved into the corner, out of the way. Olly unlocked the door and the two policemen entered the room. Mrs Browne looked over at Olly, making the zipping mouth motion with her fingers across her lips.

"Olly! You don't look very sick," Sargeant Coppers said, peering closely at Olly.

"I am sir! I mean, I was more sick earlier and I'm feeling a bit better now," said Olly, putting on his best "sick" face.

"Where is Peter?" said Sargeant Coppers, suddenly getting to the point.

Peter jumped at the sound of his name. Olly jumped too. Sargeant Coppers was not wasting any time.

"How would I know?" said Olly, looking at Mrs Browne for help. "He didn't tell me where he was going."

"Have you seen him in the last two days?" asked Sargeant Coppers.

"No," said Olly truthfully.

"Why are you having a bath if you're sick?" asked Sargeant Coppers, changing direction.

"Eh, well, I was dirty," said Olly hesitantly. "Actually, I got sick on myself and that's why I had a bath."

Sargeant Coppers peered at him suspiciously and looked around the small bathroom. His eyes followed some wet footprints that were leading over to the corner of the room, but there was no one else in the room and there was nowhere obvious to hide. He stared at the empty corner for a moment but then he turned to Mrs Browne.

"Mrs Browne," he said with a frown. "You are aware that harbouring a missing person is against the law and one could be put in prison for ten years for such a crime."

He paused, waiting for Mrs Browne to reply.

"What are you telling me that for?" said Mrs Browne weakly. "I don't know where he is." She put her hand on the wall to support herself. She felt like she was going to have a heart attack.

"Just saying, Mrs Browne," said Sargeant Coppers. "So, if you know anything, you'd better tell us."

"I don't know anything," she repeated, keeping her eyes on the ground.

"All right, Mrs Browne," said Sargeant Coppers, with a sigh. "If you think of anything, please call me."

He scribbled down his number and passed it to her. Then he turned on his heels and marched out the door. The second police man quickly followed.

"I'll be back!" he called out ominously, as he left the house.

Mrs Browne and the two boys watched with relief as the two police men left the house. They were all visibly shaken. She quickly locked the front door, went to the kitchen and sat down.

Peter put his clothes on, and they followed her into the kitchen.

"Peter," said Mrs Browne. "I have to contact your parents. You heard what the police man said. I'll be in serious trouble if you are found here. That was way too close for comfort."

"Ok," said Peter, his face falling. "When?"

"Right now," replied Mrs Browne. "The police men could be back at any time. I'll call your parents first. We can't just turn up without warning them that their son is invisible. The shock would be too much. What's their phone number?"

Peter called out the number to Mrs Browne and she picked up the phone and dialled it. Peter waited, frowning at the phone as if he hoped they wouldn't answer it.

"Hello, Mr Connor?" said Mrs Browne, brightly. "I have some good news for you. We've found Peter. He's here with me now and he's safe. You can talk to him."

She passed the phone to Peter.

"Hello Dad," said Peter, dully.

"What have you been up to?" Peter's father was shouting down the phone so loudly that Mrs Browne and Olly could hear every word that he was saying. "You are in big trouble, young man. Do you know that half the country is looking for you? We've had the police here and your mother is worried sick! If you ever do something like this again, you're on your own. You won't be welcome in this house. Do you hear me? Say something!"

"I'm sorry, Dad, I'm sorry," said Peter, looking up at Mrs Browne for help.

Mrs Browne could see that Peter was stuck for words. She took the phone back off him.

"Mr Connor, your son has been through quite a lot recently and doesn't deserve to be spoken to like that. In fact, there's something that I have to warn you about. He might not be able to go back to school."

"What?" interrupted Mr Connor, sounding most agitated. "He has to go back to school. We can't have him here. Whatever he's done, we'll pay for the damage."

"It's not that, Mr Connor," said Mrs Browne, wondering how she was going to explain the situation. "It's, well, the thing is, he's turned invisible."

"He's what?" said Mr Connor incredulously. "Don't be silly, that's not possible. It's just some silly trick."

"I'm not joking," Mrs Browne replied firmly. "He's invisible, and we can't reverse it. Look, I think the best thing is if we drive over to you now and you can see for yourself. He's your son and he needs to go home."

"Ok, drop him over then," said Mr Connor.

Mrs Browne quickly wrote down the address and said her goodbyes. What kind of a father was Mr Connor? She couldn't believe his attitude. He couldn't care less that his missing son had been found.

"Come on, boys, into the car," she said. "And Peter, put on one of Olly's jumpers and a cap, so at least they can see you."

They all set off on the journey to Peter's house. There was an air of gloom and worry coming from Peter. It was clear that he wasn't looking forward to seeing his parents.

****

Mr Connor and his wife stood in the doorway of their house, looking at the black BMW as it made its way up the driveway.

"Where is he?" Mr Connor demanded, as Mrs Browne stepped out of the car.

"Well, hello to you too!" replied Mrs Browne, sharply. "He's in the back."

The back door of the car opened, and Mr and Mrs Connor's jaws dropped as they saw - what must be - their son getting out of the car. He was wearing a green jumper and a baseball cap, but where his face should have been, there was an empty space. They could see straight through him to the grass beyond. It was the same for where his hands and legs should have been. The jumper and hat were effectively floating towards them, but making crunching noises on the gravel.

"Hello Mum," came a voice, sounding small and uncomfortable.

"I'm going to get sick," cried Mrs Connor, and she ran back into the house.

"Come here, Peter. Is that really you there?" said Mr Connor, in disbelief.

Peter walked over to him and Mr Connor felt him all over. "Peter! What have you *done*???? Do you realise how serious this is? This has got to be reversed!"

He turned to Mrs Browne. "We'll deal with this now … good bye!"

"Good bye, Peter!" called Mrs Browne. "We'll see you soon. Don't worry… things will be fine." And then she muttered to Olly. "The cheek of that rude man! He couldn't even say 'thank you'!"

"Bye, Peter," called out Olly.

"Bye Mrs Browne, bye Olly," replied Peter, with a quiver in his voice.

Chapter 21

In the meantime, not so very far away, a certain secret agent was very annoyed and very determined that he should find his scientific miracle. How could he have been so stupid as to have left the keys for the handcuffs in Peter's room? This was the most exciting and valuable asset that he'd ever come across, and he'd had to sit there as Peter just walked away from under his nose.

And then there was that disgusting "dog poo under the car handle" prank. He was sure that Peter was behind that.

When Agent Boyle had heard Peter escaping out the window, he had charged out the door after him and looked all around the front of the house in desperation. Where was he? There was absolutely no sign of anyone outside. He looked up and down the road ... nothing. Which way had he gone? He MUST find him!

He ran over to his car. As he put out his hand under the car door handle, his fingers sank into something soft and squishy. He pulled away quickly and saw that his hand was covered with something that looked like mud, but was far too smelly to be mud. It was smeared around every finger and under his fingernails. The smell was disgusting. *Oh, I'm going kill whoever did this,* thought Agent Boyle. But he didn't have time to clean up the mess. He was just going to have to drive with the poo all over his hand.

He got into the car and wildly drove up and down the road, calling out to Peter in his nicest voice, "Peter, where are you? I have sweets for you!" There was absolutely no sign of Peter. After an hour he had to give up. There was poo all over the steering wheel and all over the gear stick. The car stank, and it was now all dry and crusty. Agent Boyle was disgusted and also devastated. He almost had everything and now he had nothing. The images of fabulous wealth, fame and TV shows all crumbled in his head. He sighed, and went inside to clean up, feeling very sorry for himself.

But after a while Agent Boyle began to feel better. His car was clean, he was clean, and he had a plan of action. He was not going to let the invisible boy escape. He was going to catch him! He knew his name and he knew the name of his school. He could easily find the address of his parents. He was one hundred percent sure that the boy would contact his parents. All he had to do was wait for him at his house and grab him when no one was looking. He would bring the dog too, to make sure that he would be able to locate the boy.

Agent Boyle quickly called the school. "Mr Principal, it's Agent Boyle here. I need the address of that missing boy, Peter. I might have some information regarding his whereabouts. The Willows, Millonsford? Very good. Thank you!" And he hung up the phone.

That was easy!

****

Peter waved goodbye sadly to Olly as the car disappeared down the driveway. His father gripped him by the shoulder and directed him into the house.

As soon as they sat down at the kitchen table, the questions started. Peter answered them as best he could but of course he couldn't answer the most important questions. How had this happened? Could it be reversed?

"I just wished for it," said Peter, earnestly. "I didn't do anything else."

"Do you think I'm a fool, Peter?" said his father, angrily. "You can't turn invisible by just wishing for it. You must have taken something, like a medicine, or something from the science lab. What were you messing around with?"

"I didn't drink anything!" cried Peter. "Honestly, I just wished for it."

Mr Connor gave up and went over to the computer to see if he could find any information about invisible children on the internet.

After a while Mrs Connor appeared, looking white and upset. She avoided looking at Peter, with his missing face and hands, and busied herself instead making him a sandwich.

"I'm really sorry, mum," said Peter, quietly.

Mrs Connor jumped. "Eh, it's ok, Peter," she said, hurriedly shoving the sandwich at him and stepping away. "Here, eat this and go and watch TV. We'll work something out. Don't worry. It'll all be ok." She sounded most unconvincing.

Peter went into the sitting room and sat down to watch TV. But suddenly, out of the corner of his eye, he saw something run across the garden. It looked like a large dog. He went over to the window to get a better look, but it was gone. The garden lay still and motionless, as if he had imagined it. He went back to watching the TV and had soon forgotten all his worries when the sound of his parent's voices drifted into the sitting room, jolting him rudely back to reality.

"George, he can't stay here. He's freaking me out. Can you not send him back to boarding school? They will be able to deal with him." That was his mother's voice, whispering as loudly as she dared.

"Margaret, we have to solve this problem. We can't send him back there as he is at the moment. What would the head master think of us?"

Peter listened to the conversation in dismay and decided that he didn't want to stay in this unwelcoming house; he wanted to stay with Olly – in a house where people people actually cared for him. He sat for a moment wondering how he could persuade his parents to let him stay there instead, and then he went into the kitchen. Both parents looked up at him with guilty expressions. They obviously knew that they had been overheard.

"Peter! Do you want something? It's nearly your bedtime," said his father.

"No, I'm fine Dad. Look, it's great to see you guys again, but is there any chance I could stay at Olly's house until all this gets sorted?" said Peter as diplomatically as he could. "He can keep me updated on schoolwork."

"Olly?" said his mother. "Is that the boy who dropped you off here? Well that would be a nice idea, wouldn't it, George?" She looked up at his father with a pleading look.

"Well, we could do that, I suppose, if his mother doesn't mind," said Peter's father, his face brightening at the thought. "Yes, that would be a good idea! The first thing is to call the police station to say that you're back home, and they can call off the search. Then we'll call the school and say that you'll be absent for a while. And then we'll call Olly's mother and arrange for you to stay with her."

Peter's heart jumped with joy! Everything was working out.

"Go on up to bed, Peter," said his father. "We'll discuss it and let you know tomorrow."

"Okay - goodnight!" called Peter cheerily and he skipped upstairs to bed.

****

In the meantime, Agent Boyle was not having a good time. He had arrived at Peter's parent's house and had found a spot to hide in the garden behind a bush. But hours had passed, and he was stiff and cold. It was damp in the bushes; his clothes were wet, and he was hungry. *Why had he not brought some food?* The dog was also driving him mad. He kept running out into the garden and digging up the flower beds. He was going to give the game away if he carried on like that. He was supposed to be trained! Agent Boyle looked at his watch. It was getting late now, and he was going to have to spend the night in this bush. But despite his discomfort, he was determined not to leave without the boy; nothing else was important.

When Mrs Browne's car rolled up into the Connor's driveway he looked up with expectancy. Could this be Peter? To his delight, out from the car popped the strange sight of a floating jumper and cap. That was his boy! It had been worth the wait. Now he just had to find a way of separating him from the others and grabbing him.

After the family had entered the house, Agent Boyle watched them through the windows. He saw the boy go in the sitting room on his own to watch TV, and after an hour or so he could see him upstairs, going to bed. Maybe he could sneak into the house and grab him when everyone was asleep? *No*, he thought. *There'll be better chance tomorrow. I'll just be patient and wait for the right opportunity.*

****

The next day Peter was up bright and early. He ran downstairs to breakfast.

"Did you ring her? What did she say?" he asked his mother excitedly.

"She said it would be fine, as long as she has a written letter from us to say that it's ok," said Mrs Connor, avoiding looking at Peter.

"Great!" cried Peter, running over and giving her a big hug. "Thank you so much!"

"That's ok," she replied, patting him awkwardly on the back. "Go and get your things. We'll get going after breakfast."

Peter ran upstairs and packed a suitcase; clothes, toothbrush, shoes - everything he needed for a really long stay. He didn't plan on coming back any time soon.

As he turned to leave the room, he noticed something outside in the garden again. He went over to the window and looked out. And then his heart jumped. At the far side of the garden was a man, hiding in the bushes with a dog! Who was that? What was he doing in their garden?

The dog looked very similar to the one that Agent Boyle had in the classroom. It couldn't be him coming to get him, could it? The man was hunched over and had a hat pulled down, hiding his face, so it was impossible to know if it was Agent Boyle. But Peter wouldn't put it past him to do a dirty trick like that. A shiver of fear ran down Peter's spine. He had to get out of there quickly. If Agent Boyle knew where he lived, he wouldn't stop until he caught him again.

He ran downstairs with his suitcase. "I'm ready, Mum!" he said. "Come on, let's go!"

Mrs Connor was already sitting in the car, drumming her fingers on the steering wheel impatiently.

"Too late, sucker!" said Peter, glancing over to the bushes as he ran quickly to the car.

They drove in silence during the journey to Olly's house. Peter's mother never knew what to say to him, and Peter had a lot on his mind. If that was Agent Boyle in the garden, he was going to have to protect himself. He couldn't go around constantly looking over his shoulder, waiting for someone to kidnap him. When he got to Olly's house, he would think of a plan. Olly always had great ideas.

****

As soon as Mrs Connor pulled up in front of Olly's house, Peter jumped out of the car and ran into Mrs Browne's outstretched arms.

"Thank you so much, Mrs Browne!" he cried.

Mrs Connor looked on with a mixture of jealousy and relief. He never hugged her like that... but it would be a relief to have her house back to normal. The last few days had been most upsetting. She was a woman that followed a strict routine and she didn't like any disruptions.

"Thank you, Mrs Browne," she said, awkwardly. "I'm sure he'll have a lovely time. Be a good boy, Peter and do what your told."

She fumbled in her purse, looking for some money but to her annoyance she only found a few coins. "Here, Mrs Browne. Something for his keep," she muttered.

"Money is not necessary, Mrs Connor," said Mrs Browne, glancing at the coins. "Goodbye."

Mrs Connor turned back to her car. She couldn't wait to get out of there. The whole situation was most embarrassing. It was obvious that her son couldn't wait to get away from her and she felt uncomfortable landing Mrs Browne with the expense of looking after another boy. But Mrs Browne obviously didn't mind, so she jumped in the car, beeped the horn twice to say goodbye and sped off down the drive.

****

As soon as the car had disappeared, Olly turned to Peter. "Come on, we've put up another bed in my room. I'll show you!"

The two boys ran off to Olly's room. It was great to be back again, but Peter was worried. He had to tell Olly his concern about the strange man in the garden.

"Olly, I really think that he's coming after me. He could have followed our car here and be waiting to catch me now! What are we going to do?"

"Gosh, I don't know," replied Olly. "But don't worry - we'll make a plan, so he can't bother us ever again."

The boys plotted and planned all night in bed. Peter was afraid to leave the house and also afraid to be left alone in the house in case Agent Boyle kidnapped him.

Finally, they came up with the plan that if Agent Boyle was coming for Peter, then Peter would be waiting for him. He would lay a trap for him and the hunted would catch the hunter.

Chapter 22

If Peter had known that as he spoke, his words were a reality, he would have been even more frightened. Unknown to him, behind the wall at Olly's entrance gates, Agent Boyle was lying in wait, watching him through the green leaves of a tree. Agent Boyle knew he had to catch Peter soon, after the uncomfortable night he'd spent outside Peter's house. Not having brought any blankets or a tent, he had woken up very early that morning, cold, stiff and damp. There was no way he was going to spend another night like that.

But not long after waking up, he heard the car starting up and saw Peter's mother inside. He'd thought that maybe this would be his chance to capture Peter as it looked like the boy had been left home alone. But to his annoyance, a minute later Peter appeared with a very large suitcase and dashed into the car. Agent Boyle could have sworn that he heard him say, "Too late, sucker!"

Agent Boyle had watched them as they drove away, and had run to get his car, jumping into it with the dog and speeding off down the road with a cloud of dust blowing up behind him. He followed them at a safe distance, and when Mrs Connor's car pulled up outside a large house, he had parked his car further down the road, creeping back and watching her from behind a wall at the entrance gate.

A boy, Peters age, ran out of the house followed by a stout lady. They all chatted for a few moments; the boys, excitedly, and the adults not so agreeably, it seemed, and then Mrs Connor drove away, leaving Peter at the house with his large suitcase. Agent Boyle could see that she planned to offload him at a friend's house for a while. Well, he had other plans for Peter. He wouldn't be needing that big suitcase where Agent Boyle was going to bring him.

He watched the house with mounting excitement. He was ready for action and had everything he needed for the plan to be a success; some sleeping tablets, a bottle of chloroform, hand cuffs, a blindfold, and a gag. He was determined that he would have this boy back in his possession again by the evening. The dollar signs were starting to spring back in his mind!

Presently, he saw his chance when the mother went out in the car and the other small boy, Peter's friend, went out the back door, conveniently leaving it wide open. Agent Boyle crept around the edge of the garden, looking in the window with his binoculars. Nobody in the hall … nobody in the kitchen ... aha! There he was in the sitting room playing on the computer. Agent Boyle could see a jumper and a baseball cap and nothing where his face should be. That was him all right! He checked all around to make sure that the coast was clear, and then he sneaked into the house. He knew it was risky; he could get caught, but he was confident in his secret agent stealth tactics, and was sure he wouldn't be seen.

He crept softly down the hall to where he thought the sitting room should be. He had a small mirror on a pole with him that he used for looking around corners and he used this now before entering the room. Yes, there he was. The boy was deep in concentration, absorbed in a game and hadn't a clue that he was going to be caught in two seconds! Agent Boyle's heart started beating faster with the excitement. He carefully opened the bottle of chloroform and poured a few drops on the napkin, ready to put it over the boy's nose. With one intake of breath the boy would be unconscious and silent and CAUGHT!

Agent Boyle pushed open the door abruptly, took two steps across the room and grabbed the jumper, wrapping his other arm around the place where Peter's face should have been. But, to his horror and rage he realised it wasn't a boy in his grasp, but a jumper with a pillow underneath and a clothes hanger holding up the cap. Instantly, he knew that he had been tricked. He turned to run out of the room but then he heard the click of a key turning in the lock.

He looked around wildly. He had to get away, to jump out the window. He couldn't get caught like this - like a common robber that he had so often stalked himself. How embarrassing!

"Forget it, Agent Boyle," came the familiar voice of the boy, Peter, from the other side of the door. "The police are on their way."

Agent Boyle sat down on the chair utterly defeated. The game was up, and he had lost terribly.

But a minute later, in a final moment of desperate rage, he jumped up and threw himself at the door, smashing against it with all his weight, determined to break though it.

****

Peter and Olly watched in trepidation as the door knob rattled angrily. "Let me out!" came the voice of Agent Boyle. "How dare you, you little brats!" The door shook violently as he threw his weight against it, banging and crashing.

Initially, Peter and Olly had been delighted - their plan had worked so well. The dummy was Olly's idea and they had laughed when they had added the cap for good measure. When the boys had seen Agent Boyle approaching the house, they had hidden behind the front door and Olly had made a 999 emergency call to the police station. And as they turned the key in the lock, they had felt the thrill of success.

But now, it didn't look like it was such a good idea as they watched the hinges on the door buckle against the thundering weight.

"It's going to break, Olly," said Peter, in a panic. "He's going to get out before the police get here. What are they doing? Why are they so slow?"

But just as he spoke, a welcome sound of sirens filled the air and the garden was lit up by flashing blue lights. A moment later, three burly police men entered through the open front door.

Peter recognised the police man in the lead from his visit to Olly's house. It was Sargeant Coppers. He paused in front of Olly, and Olly pointed silently down the hallway to the locked door. From the other side of the door banging and crashing sounds could be heard, and then there was a silence.

The police men crept slowly down the hall in single file.

Sargeant Coppers turned the key quietly in the lock and then looked at the other police men.

"Ready?" he whispered. "One... two... three..." He flung the door open and all three men entered the room shouting. "You're under arrest! Put your hands in the air!"

There were more bangs and thudding of feet and then the boys could hear Agent Boyle's voice from inside the room. "What are you doing? Get your hands off me! I was just visiting!"

"Agent Boyle, you are under arrest for trespass and attempted kidnap of a child. Anything you say may be used against you in court."

"But I was just visiting!"

"Hands out and put these on."

It was Agent Boyle's turn to put on the handcuffs. A moment later, he appeared, flanked by two of the police men, one on either side, dragging him along by his handcuffed arms. Agent Boyle resisted, looking wildly at the pillow as he desperately tried to profess his innocence.

"There's an invisible boy in the house!" he spluttered. "I'm investigating it. I'm a secret agent! You can't arrest me!"

"I thought you were just visiting?"

"I just said that to stop you. But now I'm telling the truth!"

"Mr Boyle, will you please stop blathering... just stop," said Sargeant Coppers in irritation. "There's no such thing as invisible boys. Do you really think we're going to believe that? It's just a pillow."

"But it's true," howled Agent Boyle. "He's here somewhere!"

The boys giggled. That was him out of action for a while.

As the police men dragged Agent Boyle outside, Mrs Browne arrived back. She jumped out of her car and ran into the house.

"What's going on?" she panted. "Is someone hurt?"

"No, Mum," said Olly. "That's Agent Boyle they're arresting. He tried to kidnap Peter again."

"What? That man came into *my* house? He's going to regret this!"

She marched out of the house, and up to the police men who were just bundling Agent Boyle into the car. Lifting her long skirt, she kicked him hard in the shins. "Take that, you big bully!"

"Wow," said Peter to Olly. "Your mum could be on the soccer team with a kick like that!"

"That's enough. Stop that now, Mrs Browne," said Sargeant Coppers sternly, but there was a twinkle in his eye. "You come with me and tell me what happened."

The boys watched as she filled in forms and answered all their questions. Finally, the cars drove away, and Mrs Browne and the two boys were left alone again. It was strangely quiet after all the excitement.

"Boys, you did a great job!" said Mrs Browne. "I don't think he'll be bothering us again."

"Yes, it was pretty impressive team work," grinned Olly.

"Now, I've telephoned your school," continued Mrs Browne, "I've explained the situation about Peter and warned them that you don't want any questions or hassle of any kind. They're going to inform all the children so that everyone is prepared for your unusual appearance, Peter."

"Oh noooo," groaned Peter and Olly at the same time. Did she really have to bring the topic of school at this moment? What a killjoy!

"Hopefully, you won't remain like this for long," said Mrs Browne. "I've contacted a skin specialist doctor who's interested in trying to solve the problem. In the meantime, we might try putting some thick make-up on your face, Peter. That way, you won't actually be invisible."

"Really?" groaned Peter again. This was getting worse … Ladies' make-up on his face? He would get really teased about that. *That's definitely not going to stay on my face past the school gate*, he thought.

But a moment later he started to change his mind. *Maybe it will come in handy for a few disguises.* He could experiment with some new looks, with different wigs and glasses. This could turn out to be a term of fun...!

He grinned at Olly who was also grinning. The same thoughts were obviously going through his head. Or maybe not. Maybe he was just imagining Peter in class trying to explain to the boys why he had make-up on his face.

But for now, for possibly different reasons, they were both looking forward to going back to school!

THE END

Made in the USA
Coppell, TX
19 January 2021